"Did you forget something?" Olivia asked.

"No, I just figured I'd see a lady to her door," Daniel replied.

"I'm not a lady, I'm your boss," she retorted with a smile.

"I have a terrible confession to make," he said as they reached her small front porch.

She pulled her house key from her purse and looked at him cautiously. "A confession?"

He nodded. "I have to confess that from the moment my new boss showed up I've wanted to kiss her."

"You kissed me last night on the forehead." Warmth filled her cheeks as she thought of that tender kiss.

"That's not the kind of kiss I'm thinking about," he replied, and took a step closer to her.

She was playing with fire and she knew it but was unable to help herself. "Then what kind of kiss have you been thinking about?" she asked, her heartbeat speeding up.

"This kind." He pulled her into his arms and slanted his lips down to hers.

SCENE OF THE CRIME: WHO KILLED SHELLY SINCLAIR?

New York Times Bestselling Author

CARLA CASSIDY

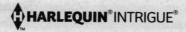

HARLEQUIN® INTRIGUE®

Recycling programs
for this product may
not exist in your area.

ISBN-13: 978-0-373-69884-4

Scene of the Crime: Who Killed Shelly Sinclair?

Copyright © 2016 by Carla Bracale

This edition published by arrangement with Harlequin Books S.A.

For questions and comments about the quality of this book, please contact us at CustomerService@Harlequin.com.

Printed in U.S.A.

Carla Cassidy is a *New York Times* bestselling author who has written more than one hundred books for Harlequin. Carla believes the only thing better than curling up with a good book to read is sitting down at the computer with a good story to write. She's looking forward to writing many more books and bringing hours of pleasure to readers.

Books by Carla Cassidy

Harlequin Intrigue

Scene of the Crime

Visit the Author Profile page at Harlequin.com for more titles.

CAST OF CHARACTERS

Sheriff Olivia Bradford—She's come to Lost Lagoon to ferret out corruption and is stunned to find herself boss to a man she'd had a one-night stand with five years before.

Deputy Daniel Carson—He's never forgotten that night he'd spent with Olivia. But now that she's reopened the Shelly Sinclair murder case, she's been threatened, and he's determined to keep her safe from the danger closing in.

Eric Baptiste—He'd fallen in love with Shelly and made plans to leave town with her. Had she decided to stay in Lost Lagoon and he killed her?

Neil Sampson—Did the handsome, charismatic city councilman have a secret that he was willing to kill to keep?

Mac Sinclair—Shelly's older brother had hated Bo McBride. Had his hatred for his sister's boyfriend boiled over into an accidental death of Shelly?

Bo McBride—Shelly's boyfriend at the time of her murder. Had he killed her in a fit of passion because she'd decided to leave him and Lost Lagoon behind?

Chapter One

Daniel Carson sat at the small desk in the Lost Lagoon sheriff station. The blinds at the windows were pulled shut, giving the office complete privacy. Outside the small glass-enclosed room, the sound of the other men in the squad room created a low buzz of constant conversation.

They would all be discussing the arrival of the new sheriff, one appointed by the state attorney to take over and root out any corruption in the department until new elections could be held in the small town.

It had been almost a month since the former sheriff, Trey Walker, and Mayor Jim Burns had been arrested for drug trafficking and attempted murder. They had been moving their product from the swamp lagoon through underground tunnels to Trey's house where it was trucked out of the state. The scandal had rocked the tiny Mississippi swamp town.

As deputy sheriff, Daniel had stepped into the position of interim acting sheriff, a job he'd never wanted and couldn't wait to end.

She should be arriving at any moment. Sheriff Olivia

Bradford, sent here from Natchez. Daniel knew nothing about her, but he expected a pit bull, a woman who not only had the ability to fire anyone at will, but who also had the power of the bigwigs of the state behind her.

It was no wonder the men were anxious to meet their new boss—anxious and more than a little bit apprehensive. Heads would roll if she found anything or anyone she didn't deem appropriate for the department. Everyone was concerned about their jobs.

Daniel checked his watch. Ten minutes after ten. He'd been told she would arrive around ten. He was probably the only one in the building who couldn't wait for her to arrive.

He leaned forward in the chair, unfastened the sheriff badge from his shirt and placed it on the top of the desk. He whirled it like a top. The spinning motion mirrored the dizzying chaos the drug scandal and the near murder of Savannah Sinclair and Daniel's best friend, Deputy Josh Griffin, had unleashed inside his head for the past month.

The newly discovered tunnels that ran beneath the entire town were still being mapped and explored by a team of volunteers under the supervision of Frank Kean, a former mayor who had stepped back into the official position when Jim Burns had been arrested. Eventually a special election would vote in a new mayor and sheriff, but not until Sheriff Olivia Bradford conducted a full investigation.

Daniel stared down at the sheriff badge. He'd be glad to give up his position of authority and return to the squad room as just another deputy. He much preferred being in the field rather than stuck behind a desk.

He became aware of the absence of conversation through the closed office door. The men in the squad room had apparently fallen silent and that could only mean one thing. Sheriff Olivia Bradford had arrived.

A firm knock fell on the office door and then it opened and she stepped in. His mind refused to work properly as he got his first look at the woman.

Lily. His head exploded with memories of a woman he'd met five years ago at a crime conference in New Orleans, a woman he'd wound up in bed with for a single night of explosive sex.

Her dark chocolate eyes widened as she gazed at him. She froze, as still as a sleeping gator on a log. It was obvious she recognized him, too.

She cleared her throat, turned and closed the door behind her and when she faced him again, her pretty features were schooled in a business-like coolness. "Sheriff Daniel Carson?" she asked.

"Former sheriff now that you've arrived," he replied and got up from the desk. Okay, so they were going to pretend that they didn't know each other. They were going to act as if that night five years ago hadn't happened.

"I'm Sheriff Olivia Bradford," she replied, a statement that was unnecessary.

"And you're here to take over for me." He pointed to the badge on the desk. He walked around the desk and she made her way behind it and sank down.

She hadn't changed much in the time since he'd last seen her. Her dark brown eyes were still pools of mystery and her long black hair was caught in a low ponytail at the nape of her neck.

That night it had been loose and silky in his fingers and her eyes had glowed with desire. The khaki uniform she wore couldn't hide the thrust of her breasts, her slender waist or her long shapely legs.

Tangled sheets, soft skin against his and low, husky moans, the memories tumbled over themselves in his brain and he desperately tried to shove them away.

She sat down and motioned him into one of the two straight-backed chairs in front of the desk. As he sat, she grabbed the badge from the top of the desk and pinned it onto her breast pocket.

When she looked at him once again her eyes were flat and cool. She appeared the consummate professional. "I've been filled in about the issues with the former sheriff and mayor. I'm sure you have heard that my job here is to clean up any further corruption that might linger in the department. I also would like to go through any crime records for the past five years or so, since Trey Walker was sheriff."

"I'll see to it that you get whatever you need," he replied. It was as if he was having a little bit of an out-of-body experience as he tried to process the woman he'd known intimately and briefly before and the woman who now sat across from him.

"I hope my taking over doesn't stir up any resentment with you."

He laughed drily. "Trust me, I couldn't wait to get rid of this position. I never had any desire to be sheriff. It was just something that got thrust on me due to unforeseen circumstances."

"Good, although my job here isn't to make friends with anyone." She spoke the words with a slight upthrust of her chin. "I don't know how long I'll be here, but my basic job is an internal investigation into both the way crimes were handled under Sheriff Walker and to look at the current employees and see if there are more bad players in the department."

"I'm sure you'll find that most of us are all working on the same page," he replied. Throughout the years, had she ever thought about that night with him? He'd certainly been haunted off and on with memories and wondering whatever happened to the passionate woman he'd met in a bar.

He noticed the gold wedding band on her finger. So, she was married. A faint disappointment winged through him, surprising him. He had no interest in marriage, and certainly that single night they had shared hadn't grown into any kind of a relationship with her.

She was his boss now, and both the wedding ring on her finger and the coolness in her eyes let him know the brief encounter he'd shared with her wouldn't absolve him from intense scrutiny in her investigation. Not that he would ever mess around with a married woman and not that he expected to be treated any differently from any of the other men.

They'd had a one-night hookup years ago and hadn't

seen each other again. Hell, he hadn't even known her real full name. He'd only known her as Lily.

"I'd like to have a meeting with all the deputies at two this afternoon. Could you arrange that for me?" she asked, breaking into his wayward thoughts.

"Yes, I'll see to it that all of the men are here at that time. We have a nineteen-man work force. In the meantime, do you want me to start gathering the crime files? I'm assuming the employment records are in there." He gestured to a nearby file cabinet.

"Yes, please get me the files. I don't want to waste any time." She stood and walked to the file cabinet and Daniel took that as a dismissal.

He left the office and closed the door behind him. Half a dozen pairs of eyes were staring at him. He ignored them all and walked over to the desk where he had sat a month ago as a deputy.

As he eased down in his chair, several of the other deputies surrounded him. "What's she like?" Deputy Josh Griffin asked.

"She looked like a mean witch when she walked in," Ray McClure exclaimed. "A great-looking mean witch," he added with a smirk.

Daniel held up a hand to silence any further questioning from any of them. "If you thought she was going to be a soft touch because she's a woman, get that thought right out of your head. I suggest you all be on your toes and conduct yourselves as professionals. My gut feeling is that she's going to be tough as nails and none of us are secure in our jobs."

It was a sober group of men who returned to their desks. Daniel stared down at his blotter, still trying to process that Olivia Bradford was the young woman he'd known for a night as hot, sexy Lily.

He pulled his cell phone out of his pocket. He had calls to make to the men who weren't in to let them know a full staff meeting had been called for two that afternoon.

After that he would be busy pulling files from the small room dedicated to files and evidence in the back of the building.

While he was completing these tasks, he had to figure out a way to forget that he'd ever known, even briefly, a sexy, passionate woman named Lily.

OLIVIA GRABBED THE employment files for the men on the force and then sank back down at the desk. She'd nearly lost it when she'd walked into the office and seen that man again.

Daniel. She'd never expected to run into him after all these years. Shock still washed over her as she thought of the handsome dark-haired, green-eyed man.

That night in New Orleans she'd been a twenty-five-year-old deputy who had lost her partner and good friend in a shoot-out the week before. She hadn't wanted to attend the conference but her boss had insisted that it would be good for her to get away from Natchez and her grief.

She'd kept to herself during the four-day event, venturing out to a bar near the hotel only on the final night in town. She hadn't been looking for company. She'd wanted only to drown her grief in margaritas and then return to the hotel to pack and prepare to leave early the next morning.

She hadn't expected Daniel to sit next to her, and she certainly hadn't anticipated finding succor for her grief in his arms. It had been a foolish, impulsive night, and hopefully he had no idea how the unexpected sight of him had shaken her to her very core.

She shoved away thoughts of Daniel and instead spent the next hour focused on the employment records for the eighteen men and one woman who comprised the law enforcement in Lost Lagoon, Mississippi.

Most of the deputies had been born and raised in Lost Lagoon, although there were a few who had been hired in from other towns. There were no disciplinary notes, nothing to indicate that Trey Walker had endured any issues with any of them.

But Trey Walker had proven himself to be a crook and a lowlife, and she didn't trust his record keeping. At noon she pulled out a chicken salad sandwich that her mother had made for her before she'd left their rental home that morning.

Although Olivia had arrived in town two days earlier, she'd spent those days turning a renovated shanty on the swamp side of town into a livable space for the duration of her stay.

The place had come partially furnished, but Olivia had pulled a trailer behind her car, which had carried the extra furnishing and personal items to make their stay here as comfortable as possible.

She'd just finished her sandwich when a knock sounded on the door. She called for the person to come in and Daniel entered carrying a box. He set it on her desk.

"That's the files on all the crimes that have occurred for the last five years," he said.

She eyed the box dubiously. "That's it?"

He cast her a smile that instantly shot a spark of heat in her. She'd forgotten about that sexy smile of his. "We're a small town. Except for the last couple of months, there's been very little crime in Lost Lagoon."

She looked back at the box, unwilling to hold eye contact with him while that smile still lingered on his features. "That would be a daily box for Natchez."

"You aren't in Natchez anymore. I got hold of all the officers and they will be here at two for a meeting."

She finally glanced back up at him. "Thank you, I appreciate the cooperation."

He nodded and then left the office. She stared at the box and then set it down next to the desk. She'd take it home with her to look at thoroughly that evening. In the meantime, she had to gather her thoughts for the meeting that was to take place in a little more than an hour.

The responsibility that had been placed on her shoulders was heavy, and she was aware that many eyes would be on her work here. She wasn't afraid of hard work and she didn't worry about the scrutiny.

She had worked long and hard to climb the ranks in

the Natchez Sheriff Department. She'd taken on cases nobody else wanted, worked harder and longer than anyone one else and had garnered not only a stellar reputation, but also dozens of honors and awards.

She wasn't about to let this temporary stint in Lost Lagoon ruin her reputation. She would do her job here and do it well.

It was exactly two o'clock when she stood in the front of a conference room where nineteen deputies sat in chairs before her. She wasn't nervous—rather, she was determined that all of the men would not only respect her, but also fear her just a little bit.

There was only one female deputy and she sat in the front row. According to the employment records she was forty-three-year-old Emma Carpenter and had worked as a deputy for the past ten years.

"Good afternoon," Olivia began briskly. "As all of you probably know by now, I'm Sheriff Olivia Bradford and I'm here to ferret out any further corruption that might be in this department. Consider yourself on notice that I'll be looking not only at your work performance here but potentially investigating your personal lives, as well."

Her words were met with a grumble of discontent. She ignored it. As she had told Daniel earlier, she wasn't here to make friends.

"Over the next couple of days, I'll be meeting with each of you individually," she continued.

"Looking for snitches," a voice in the back muttered.

She identified the man who had spoken as a small,

wiry officer with ferret-like features. She stared at him for a long, uncomfortable moment, until he broke eye contact with her and looked down at the floor.

"I'm not looking for snitches. I'll be getting input from each of you on how to make this department run more efficiently and I'll also be looking for anyone who isn't working in the best interest of law enforcement." She was aware of the warning in her voice and she also knew her tough words wouldn't make her the most popular person in the room.

Her gaze fell on Daniel in the second row. As deputy sheriff he would have worked closely with Trey Walker. Was he the upright, moral man she'd like him to be, or did he hide secrets that would put them at odds?

Time would tell. She'd already identified ferret-face as a potential troublemaker, and she had a feeling by reading Emma Carpenter's body language that the woman was potentially a suck-up, probably assuming since they were both women they'd share some kind of special relationship.

When Olivia put on her badge, she was neither male nor female, she was simply an officer of the law. She didn't like suck-ups and she definitely didn't like troublemakers.

She finished the meeting by instructing everyone to go about their business as usual and then returned to her office and closed the door.

For the next couple of hours, Olivia continued to study the background checks and any other pertinent information that was in the files about the men and the one woman who would be working for her.

It was her task to find out if any of those lawmen had also been involved in the drug-trafficking scheme. It was hard to believe that Trey Walker and Jim Burns had acted all alone, but it was possible nobody in the sheriff's department had known anything about it. She hoped that was the case. There was nothing she hated worse than a dirty deputy.

Even as she tried to stay focused on the paperwork in front of her, visions of Daniel intruded again and again, breaking her concentration.

She was still stunned that fate had brought them together again. Thankfully, he hadn't mentioned the night in New Orleans when they'd sat in the bar and talked about jazz music and Mardi Gras. She'd seen him before at the conference, so she knew he was a lawman somewhere, but neither of them had talked about where they worked or where they were from.

They'd had drink after drink and hadn't mentioned crime or their work. Their conversation had been superficial and flirtatious, just what she'd needed to escape the grip of nearly overwhelming grief.

What happened after they'd left the bar and gone to his hotel room had been crazy and wild and wonderful, but she'd left town early the next morning never dreaming that she'd ever see him again.

It was just after five when she decided to call it a day. She wanted to spend most of the evening going through the box of files that should hold not only information about the recent arrests of Trey Walker and Jim Burns, but also any crime investigations that had occurred under Walker's watch.

She grabbed her purse and the box and headed out of the office. She had only taken a couple of steps into the squad room when Daniel jumped up from his desk and took the box from her. "I'll carry it to your car," he said.

"Thanks," she replied. Tension filled her. Did he intend to mention that night once they stepped out of the station and were all alone? She didn't want to talk about it. She didn't even want it mentioned. It had been an anomaly and had nothing to do with who she was or had been.

He led her to the back door of the building that would open up on the parking lot. "Have you gotten settled in okay here in town?" he asked as they stepped outside and into the late August heat.

"I've rented one of the renovated places along the swamp, and, yes, I'm settled in just fine." She walked briskly toward her car.

"Have you had a chance to look around town?"

"Not really, although I did meet with Mayor Frank Kean yesterday and he assured me his full cooperation while I'm here. I'm hoping to do some sightseeing in the next day or two." They reached her car and she opened the passenger door to allow him to set the box inside.

"The Lost Lagoon Café is a great place to eat, but I'd stay away from the diner. George's Diner is actually just a hamburger joint, but if you want really good food then I'd recommend Jimmy's Place. It's a bar and grill that serves great food."

"Thanks for the information, but I will probably eat at home most of the time."

He placed the box in the passenger seat and she closed the door and hurried around to the driver door. "I'll see you in the morning," she said and before he could say anything else she slid into the seat and closed the door.

As she pulled away, she glanced in her rearview mirror. He stood in the same place, a tall, ridiculously handsome man watching her leave.

She'd been instantly attracted to him when they'd met in the bar and she was surprised to realize that after all this time she was still attracted to him.

She squeezed the steering wheel more tightly. No matter how attracted she was to Daniel and he to her, nothing would come of it. There was too much to lose.

Her tension eased the moment she pulled into the short driveway in front of the small bungalow-type house. It was painted a bright yellow, not only setting it off from the green of the swamp land behind it, but also making for a bit of cheer among the row of ramshackle and deserted shanties that lined the street. Only a few of the shanties had been renovated and appeared like gems among the others.

She got out of the car and went around and grabbed the box from the passenger seat. She hadn't even made it to the door when it opened and her mother smiled at her.

Rose Christie had been a godsend over the last couple of years. Olivia had always been close to her mother, but their relationship had deepened when Olivia's father had died of an unexpected heart attack seven years ago.

Rose opened the door wider to allow Olivia to walk into the tiny living room that held the futon where Olivia slept, an upholstered rocking chair and a small television.

The kitchen area was little more than a row of the necessary appliances with room for a small round table and chairs.

Olivia had just set the box of files on the top of the table and taken off her gun belt, which went on the top of one of the kitchen cabinets, when a squeal came from one of the two bedrooms. Olivia crouched down and braced herself as a dark-haired, green-eyed four-year-old came barreling toward her.

"Mommy, you're home!" She threw herself into Olivia's awaiting arms.

Olivia pulled her daughter close enough that she could nuzzle her sweet little neck. "Ah, nothing smells better than my Lily flower."

Lily giggled and hugged Olivia tight. "Silly Mommy, Nanny's sugar cookies smell better than a flower."

"Not better than my Lily flower," Olivia said as the two broke apart. "Come sit and tell me what you did today."

Olivia and Lily sat side by side on the futon while Rose bustled in the kitchen to prepare dinner. "I played dolls and then Nanny and I watched a movie."

As Olivia watched and listened to her beautiful

daughter relay the events of her day, her heart swelled with love.

Unexpected and unplanned, Lily had added a richness, a joy in Olivia's life that she'd never expected to have. She was bright and more than a little precocious, and now Olivia couldn't imagine her life without Lily.

By eight thirty dinner had been eaten, Lily's bath was complete and she was in bed in one of the two bedrooms. Olivia's mother had retired to the other bedroom, leaving Olivia alone with a box of files and conflicting thoughts she'd never believed she'd have to entertain.

She'd never thought the day would come when she'd meet the man who had fathered Lily. She'd never considered what she might do if she did run into him again.

Daniel.

She was his boss and he was the father of her child. Should she tell him about Lily or should she keep the secret to herself? What was the right thing to do for everyone involved?

She didn't know the answer.

Hoping the right answer would eventually present itself to her, she opened the box of files and pulled out the first one.

Chapter Two

Daniel had spent a restless night plagued by dreams of New Orleans and the passionate woman who'd come with him back to his hotel room from the bar. He'd finally awakened before dawn and after a shower and two cups of coffee, he thought he was prepared to face the woman who was now his boss.

Lily had only been a dream, but Olivia Bradford had already shown herself to be a formidable figure. Daniel wasn't afraid of her digging into his professional or personal life. He'd never even taken a free cup of coffee from the café in his position as deputy and as temporary sheriff. He had nothing to hide, but there were several deputies he knew who didn't hold themselves to the same standards.

Olivia appeared to be the type who would leave no stone unturned both in her internal investigation and any others that might present themselves, due to Trey Walker's dictatorial style and lack of real investigations during his reign as sheriff.

Daniel arrived at the station at six forty-five ready for roll call at seven o'clock. He was unsurprised that

Olivia was already in the office. He had a feeling that she was the type of woman who wouldn't abide anything but strict punctuality.

Apparently, the men knew that, too. Even the deputies who had often been stragglers to roll call were all present, uniforms neat and eyes clear.

Five deputies worked the day shift and then five worked the evening shift until midnight, then five more were on duty from midnight until eight in the morning. The extra four worked shifts when the others had days off.

Daniel had worked the night shift until he'd become sheriff and then had changed to the day shift. He assumed he would continue his day shift even now that Olivia was here.

At precisely seven the five men working the day shift were in the conference room and Olivia walked in. Today she was clad in a pair of black slacks, a crisp white short-sleeved blouse with her badge pinned to the blouse's pocket and her gun belt around her waist.

Her hair was pulled back and her makeup minimal. She held a file in her hand. "Good morning," she said. "The first thing I'd like for you to do is stand up one at a time and state your name."

Daniel stood up first, followed by Josh Griffin, Wes Stiller, Ray McClure and Malcolm Appleton. Daniel and Josh were particularly close, having been friends for years, and they had worked together to bring down Trey and Jim.

Once they had all introduced themselves, Olivia held

up the file in her hand into the air. "I spent most of the night going through criminal file records for the last five years and one in particular captured my attention."

Daniel knew immediately which file she held in her hand. It was woefully thin and unsolved. Guilt immediately pooled in his gut as he and Josh exchanged a quick glance.

"Who killed Shelly Sinclair?" Olivia's question hung in the air for a long, pregnant moment before she continued. "This is a two-year-old unsolved murder case and as far as I can tell, very little was done at the time of her murder in the way of an investigation." She placed the file down on the table in front of her.

"That's because at the time of the murder we knew who had committed it," Ray said. "Bo McBride killed Shelly. He was her boyfriend at the time."

Olivia frowned. "Then why isn't the case closed?"

"We couldn't find the evidence necessary to make the arrest," Wes said.

"Is there another file someplace? What I have here surely doesn't contain all of the interviews and statements of people who might have been involved in the case." Olivia's dark eyes radiated confusion as she looked at each of the men.

"A good solid investigation was never done," Daniel said as the guilt knot in his gut twisted tighter.

"I don't understand," Olivia replied.

"That's because you weren't working for Trey Walker," Josh added. Daniel knew Josh had suffered just as much guilt as Daniel had with the way the case had been shunted aside. "Trey had made up his mind that Bo was guilty and he made it clear that any of us who wanted to investigate further did so at the risk of our jobs."

Olivia's lush lips pressed together in a sign of obvious disapproval. "You have an unsolved murder that's now become a cold case and a shoddy investigation at best at the time the murder occurred. We're going to reopen this case and get it solved. Daniel, I'd like to see you in my office and the rest of you get back to your usual duties."

"What a waste of time," Ray grumbled when Olivia had left the room. "Everyone knows that Bo did it. It's not our fault that we couldn't prove it."

"Not everyone is so certain that Bo was responsible," Josh replied.

That's the last of the conversation Daniel heard as he left the room to head to Olivia's office. He was glad that she was being proactive in the case of Shelly's murder. The unsolved case had been like a stain on Daniel's soul for far too long.

He knocked on the door and then entered the office where she gestured him into one of the chairs in front of her desk.

"I read what little was in the file, but I want you to tell me about Shelly Sinclair and her death," she said.

Daniel nodded and tried to school his thoughts. The scent of a lilac-based perfume filled the air. He hadn't noticed it yesterday, but he remembered it from the night they had hooked up in New Orleans. He had found it dizzyingly intoxicating then and it still affected him on some primal level.

"Daniel?"

Her voice yanked him out of the past and to the present.

"Sorry...yes, about Shelly. She was found floating in the lagoon at the south end of town. She'd been strangled. The area has a bench and some bushes, and from the scene it appeared some kind of a struggle had ensued. Her purse and phone was found on the bench, but her engagement ring was missing and has never been found."

"Now tell me about Bo McBride."

Daniel shifted positions in his chair, oddly disappointed that her eyes held nothing but professional curiosity about a crime. Of course, that was how it should be. A married woman shouldn't be interested in the five years that had passed since a hot hookup had occurred.

"At the time of the murder, Bo owned the place that is now Jimmy's Place. Bo and Shelly had been a couple since junior high school and it was just assumed that eventually they'd get married. They often met at the bench by the lagoon late at night before Shelly started her night shift working as the clerk in The Pirate's Inn. When Shelly wound up dead it was only natural that Bo would be one of the prime suspects."

"And from what I read in the file, his alibi was that he was at home sick with the flu on the night that Shelly was murdered."

"And the last text message on Shelly's phone was

from Bo telling her he was ill and couldn't meet her that night," Daniel replied.

Olivia shuffled through the few papers that were in the file. "And no other suspects were pursued? All I see in here are interviews of Shelly's sister, Savannah, her brother, Mac, their parents and a couple of Shelly's friends. Is there anything more you can tell me that isn't in this file?"

"Several things have come to light in the last couple of months. Shelly told some of her friends that she was in a sticky situation, but we never managed to figure out what that meant. While we were investigating the attacks on Shelly's sister, Savannah, we discovered that Eric Baptiste had become friendly with Shelly right before her death, a detail we never knew during the initial investigation."

Olivia held up her hand to stop him. "I'm already confused by names and incidents I know nothing about. Obviously you can't completely update me in a brief talk right now." She frowned thoughtfully. "What I'd like you to do is head up a four-man task force and focus efforts on starting this investigation all over again from the very beginning."

"I'd be glad to do that. I always felt like Bo was an easy scapegoat and the crime wasn't investigated right from the start. Is there anyone in particular you want on the task force?" he asked.

She shook her head, her dark hair shining richly in the light flooding in from the windows behind her desk. "You know the men better than I do and you know who you'll work best with. I just want go-getters, men who want to work hard and close this case with a killer behind bars."

She narrowed her eyes. "I want this cleaned up before I leave here."

There was nothing of Lily in the hard-eyed woman seated across from him. "We'll get it cleaned up," he said, hoping his words of confidence would somehow soften her features.

They didn't. Instead, in an effort to get a small glimpse of the woman he'd briefly known, he changed the subject. "I couldn't help but notice the wedding ring on your finger. I'm glad that you found somebody important in your life."

She stared down at the band for a long moment and then looked back at him, her eyes shuttered and unreadable. "I got married to a wonderful man, had a daughter and then last year he died. It's just my mother, my daughter and me now."

"Oh, I'm so sorry." That's what you get for trying to take the conversation to a personal level, he thought.

She frowned. "I'm not the first young widow and I won't be the last. What's important to me now is my family's well-being and my work. And now, don't you have a task force to pull together?" She raised a perfectly arched eyebrow and glanced toward the door.

Daniel beat feet to the door and it was only when he was back at his desk that he processed what he'd just learned about her. She wasn't married. She was a widow.

Although he was sorry that she'd lost her husband, he wasn't sorry that she was single. Right now the night they had spent together was like a white elephant in the room whenever they were alone together.

Sooner or later he was going to bring it up. He was going to have to talk about it. Sooner or later, as crazy as he might be, he hoped that just maybe there might be a repeat of that night in their future.

OVER THE NEXT two days, the task force was pulled together and assigned to work from a small conference room in the back of the building.

Daniel had chosen Josh Griffin, Wes Stiller and Derrick Bream as his team. It was obvious the men had a good relationship and equally obvious, as Olivia had observed the deputies over the last two days, that Daniel was a natural-born leader. All of the men respected and looked up to him.

Olivia had spent most of the two days interviewing the deputies who worked for her and finishing up going through case files of crimes that had been handled by Trey Walker.

Daniel had been right; for the most part other than during the last couple of months, Lost Lagoon had been relatively free of any serious crimes. Oh, there had been the usual domestic calls and shoplifting... Petty crimes that had been resolved immediately.

She'd arrived in her official capacity on Monday morning and by Wednesday evening she had learned that everyone in Lost Lagoon seemed to move at a

slower pace than anywhere else in the world. She'd discovered that the town was rich in pirate lore and that a new amusement park being built on a ridge just above the town had the business owners excited about new commerce.

It was after seven when she packed up to leave to go home. She'd already called her mother to tell her to go ahead and feed Lily and get her ready for bed.

She was surprised to leave the office and see Daniel at his desk. She'd assumed he'd gone home at four when he was off duty.

"I thought you'd have left by now. Don't you have a family to get home to?" she asked.

He reared back in his chair, looking as fresh and alert as he had that morning. "No wife, no family and no desire for either. I'm a confirmed bachelor," he said. "I assume you're headed home?"

"Eventually, but before that I want to go to the scene of Shelly's murder. I haven't really gotten out and about town much and I just want to get a feel for where the crime took place."

Daniel frowned. "I'd rather you not go there by yourself. How about I drive there and you follow me? I can give you a better idea of what things looked like on that night."

"I can't ask you to do that," she protested.

"You didn't. I offered. Besides, it's my job to assist you." He stood as if it were settled. "I was ready to knock off for the night anyway."

Minutes later Olivia followed behind Daniel's patrol car toward the south end of town. They traveled on Main Street, and as she drove she glanced at the various businesses that lined the streets.

So far she'd only gone from the station to her home on the west side of town. She hadn't ventured into the heart of Lost Lagoon. On one side of the street she noticed an ice cream parlor and made a note to be sure and visit it with her mother and Lily. Lily loved ice cream.

Lily. If she'd been conflicted at all about telling Daniel that their night of passion had resulted in a daughter for him, her conflict had been resolved when he'd said he had no desire for a wife or a family and that he was a confirmed bachelor.

She focused back on her surroundings. On one corner a shop held a large sign that indicated it was Mama Baptiste's Apothecary and Gift Shop and further down the road was a two-story hotel named The Pirate's Inn. In between were shops catering to tourists, a dress boutique and Jimmy's Place where the parking spaces in front of the three-story building were filled with various makes and models of vehicles.

Olivia's stomach rumbled as she thought of all the people inside enjoying a meal. She'd skipped lunch that day and although she knew Rose would have kept something for her to zap in the microwave for dinner, her stomach was ready to be fed as soon as possible.

While they continued on, the buildings ended and Main Street joined an outer road that she knew circled around the entire town.

Olivia followed him onto the outer road and then

when he stopped and pulled to the curb, she did the same. On the opposite side of the road in the near distance was a row of bushes broken only by a stone bench.

Daniel got out of his car and she followed suit. Here the smell of the swamp was thick in the humid air. The scent of tangled musty foliage battled with a fishy smell, and the humidity was thick enough to cut with a knife.

Daniel joined her by the side of her car. "Bo worked the night shift at Bo's Place and Shelly worked the night shift at The Pirate's Inn. Before she went into work, Bo often sneaked away and the two of them would meet here for a few minutes before they each returned to work."

"So Shelly showed up that night, but according to the message that she got from Bo, he didn't come." Olivia stared at the bench where a young, beautiful woman had spent the last minutes of her life. Who had met Shelly here in the middle of the night and strangled her to death then threw her body in the nearby lagoon?

They crossed the street. Beyond the bushes and the stone bench was a grassy area that ran from one edge of the swampy growth to the other side, and beyond that the lagoon water sparkled darkly in the waning sunlight.

"No evidence was found?" Olivia asked.

"The bushes on the left side of the bench were trampled down, indicating that the struggle occurred there, but we didn't find anything in the way of evidence." His voice held a wealth of frustration.

"From the minute I read this file, I've been haunted by her," Olivia said softly.

"You aren't the only one. I've spent two years with her ghost haunting my dreams, begging for justice. In the last year, Shelly's sister, Savannah, kept her sister relevant by dressing up like a ghost and walking on the grassy area just in front of the lagoon."

Olivia looked at him in surprise. "Really?"

"On Friday nights teenagers would gather and hide behind the bushes, waiting for the ghost of Shelly to appear. Savannah used a tunnel that runs from her backyard to the base of a tree." He pointed to the right of the grassy area where a cypress tree rose up. "She'd wear some gauzy white dress with a flashlight tied to her waist beneath to give her a ghostly glow. She'd walk across to the other side where a cave led back to the tunnel that would take her home."

"Why would she do such a thing?" Olivia asked, wanting to know all the ins and outs of this case.

Daniel shoved his hands in his pockets and stared at the dark lagoon water. He appeared haunted, his eyes fixed in the distance and his posture one of faint defeat.

"When Shelly was buried, Savannah's parents moved away and left her and her brother, Mac, the family house. Mac married and moved out soon after that. According to Shelly, she wasn't allowed to speak of her sister, either to her parents or to her brother. She did her ghostly walks to hear the teenagers behind the bushes gasp and shout out Shelly's name. It was her way of keeping her sister alive."

He pulled his hands from his pockets and turned back to gaze at Olivia. "Thankfully, Josh caught on to

what she was doing and with his love she's healing. But she needs closure. She needs her sister's killer behind bars to fully embrace the life she's building with Josh."

"Tomorrow I'd like you to go with me to interview Bo McBride. I know small towns and that often people are hostile or suspicious of strangers. I think I'll get more answers if you're with me."

Daniel nodded. "Just tell me when and I'll be glad to go with you."

Olivia walked forward and sat on the bench, as if she could somehow pick up something from the horror of the crime that had happened so long ago.

It was darker here, the sinking sun unable to penetrate the shadows formed by the swamp vegetation and the trees with thick Spanish moss dripping from their branches.

Daniel sat next to her. His spicy cologne was familiar as it wafted to her. It wasn't just a familiar scent she'd noticed over the last couple of days, but one she remembered from a night that shouldn't have happened. It was a night that should have been erased from her memory bank long ago.

"Tell me about Bo McBride," she said in an effort to keep away memories that had no place in her head.

"Bo was one of the golden boys in town. He was liked and respected by everyone. He was handsome and had a beautiful girlfriend. His business was extremely successful and at least on the surface it appeared he had the world by the tail."

"Do you think he killed Shelly?"

His features were dappled by shadows and his eyes glowed silvery green in the falling of twilight. They had glowed like that when he'd taken possession of her body. Darn it, she had to stop remembering him naked and filled with desire for her.

He raked a hand through his thick short hair and leaned back against the bench. "Do I think Bo killed Shelly? My gut instinct is that he didn't."

"And how good is your gut instinct?"

He grinned at her, his perfect white teeth flashing bright. "Better than most, but in this case I guess time and more investigation will tell us if it's on the money."

"Who found her body? I didn't see anything in the report."

"An early morning jogger named Tom Dempsey. Tom is sixty-seven years old and jogs at odd times of the day and night. It was four in the morning when he saw Shelly floating in the swamp and called it in. Thankfully, we managed to retrieve her before any gators or other wildlife got to her."

Olivia had been involved in many homicide cases in Natchez, but for some reason the case of Shelly Sinclair was hitting her hard. She rose from the bench, not wanting to sit another minute in this place of death.

Daniel stood, as well. "I have a favor to ask you," she said as they walked back to their cars. She paused and gazed up at him. "I've been watching the way you interact among the men and it's obvious they look up to you. What I need to know is if I can trust you completely?"

She held his gaze steadily. She might be making a mistake, but she needed somebody on the inside, somebody who had worked closely with the other men in the department.

She had no real reason to trust Daniel. A single night in bed certainly wasn't the basis to build trust on, but her gut instinct told her he was the one man in the department who was an upright, by-the-book lawman.

"Of course you can trust me completely," he replied. The earnestness in his eyes comforted her.

"Then what I'd like to do is meet you for coffee one evening soon at the café and have a talk about some of your fellow officers," she said.

He frowned. "I'd really rather not do that at the café where people can see us together or might overhear the conversation. I don't want the men to think I'm being a snitch."

"Of course, I didn't think about that."

"Why don't you follow me to my place now and we can talk privately there?"

Olivia thought about all the questions she had about some of the deputies. "Okay," she agreed a bit reluctantly.

It was only when she was back in her car and following him to his place that she thought this might be a bad idea. First and foremost she was running only on a gut instinct and his word that he was trustworthy.

More important, she feared that in the privacy of his

home he might bring up that night they'd shared five years ago, a night she'd spent the last five years trying desperately to forget.

Chapter Three

He'd been vaguely surprised when Olivia had agreed to come to his home to talk, but as he pulled into the driveway he punched the garage door opener that would open both sides of the double garage and she apparently understood that he intended for her to pull in next to him.

No need for anyone to see her car parked outside his house. It was one thing for them to be seen together in an official capacity, but another altogether for them to be together in their off-duty hours.

The last thing she would want was any kind of gossip to start up about her, and there was no reason to invite it by being careless at this point in time.

When she was parked inside and out of her car, he punched the button to close the doors behind them. "Call me paranoid," he said when they were both out of the cars. "I just think it best if people don't know we have any kind of a relationship outside of work hours."

"I appreciate it and I agree."

When he opened the door that led from the garage into the kitchen, he was grateful that by nature he was a neat and tidy man. He didn't have to worry about errant boxers dangling off light fixtures or beer bottles lined up like soldiers awaiting a trip to the trash. He gestured her to the round oak kitchen table and then moved to the counter to make a pot of coffee.

"Nice house," she said as she sat. "Big for a man who told me he has no desire for a wife or a family."

"Thanks, it really is more than I need but it was a foreclosure and I couldn't resist the great price. It needed a little cosmetic TLC, and I've managed to finish it all up."

The coffee began to brew and he turned and leaned against the cabinet to face her. "Don't worry, I didn't buy it with ill-gotten gains."

"That never crossed my mind. From reading the records, I know that you and Josh Griffin were instrumental in the arrest of Trey Walker and Jim Burns."

"It was mostly Josh. Savannah had been attacked and Josh hunted through the underground tunnels to see if he could find any evidence. What he found was an entrance that led up to Walker's garage filled with meth."

"So you trust Josh."

"With my life," he replied easily. "He and I are not only fellow deputies, we're also close friends." He had the ridiculous impulse to walk over to her and pull off the clasp from the nape of her neck that held her beautiful long hair captive.

He turned back to the cabinet and pulled out two cups. "Cream or sugar or both?" he asked.

"Just black is fine," she replied. "What about Emma Carpenter? Is she a good deputy?"

It was obvious this private meeting was just as she'd indicated it would be, an opportunity for her to pick his brains about his coworkers. He poured their coffee and then joined her at the table.

"Emma is a hard worker. She's thoughtful and meticulous and I'd trust her under any circumstances."

Olivia cupped her hands around her coffee mug. "I'm just trying to get an idea of the people who work here for the department. The employment files were relatively inadequate as far as any notes of discipline or commendations anyone might have received."

"For the most part we're a good team," he said.

"For the most part…" she echoed with a raise of a dark brow.

Daniel sighed. "I don't want to believe that any of the other officers had anything to do with the drug-trafficking issue."

"I sense a *but* on the end of that sentence."

He smiled ruefully. "But there are a couple of men I don't completely trust."

She leaned forward and he caught a whiff of that lilac fresh spring scent that had once driven him half-mad with desire for her. It still affected him on a visceral level, evoking unwanted memories of the night they'd shared.

"Who don't you trust?" she asked.

He watched her lips move and remembered the fiery kisses they'd shared. He mentally shook himself and focused on the topic at hand. "I don't want you to think that I'm some kind of snitch, but you do have a right to know potential problems within the department."

She took a sip of her coffee, her eyes dark and unfathomable over the rim of the cup. "Give me names," she said as she lowered her cup back to the table.

"Ray McClure. He was very close to Walker, but insists he had no idea what was going on when it came to the drugs flowing in and out of town. He also seemed particularly eager to point a finger at Bo for the murder of Shelly."

"I'd already identified him as an issue," she admitted. "He's lazy and borders on insubordination. Do you think he might have had something to do with Shelly's murder?"

"I doubt it. I think he was just following Trey's lead in proclaiming Bo guilty in order to please Trey and to not have to do the work of a real investigation."

"Who else?"

Daniel thought of all the men he worked with on a daily basis. "Randy Fowler isn't somebody I'd trust to have my back. He works the night shift and he recently moved his mother into a fairly pricey nursing home in Jackson. He'd bitched about the cost for months before he moved her, but now suddenly he's not complaining anymore."

"Was he particularly close to Walker?"

Daniel shook his head. "Not that any of us noticed, but he and his wife were friendly with Jim Burns."

"Is there anyone else that you can think of?"

"Not really. I've worked with these men for years,

and in most cases I grew up with them. Ray McClure is a local. He was a surly and lazy kid who never changed. As far as Randy Fowler goes, he isn't a local, but was hired in from Tupelo about six years ago. He keeps himself a bit distant from the other men."

He took a drink of his coffee and eyed her intently. "Are we ever going to talk about that night in New Orleans?"

She froze and a faint pink color filled her cheeks. "I was hoping we wouldn't."

"I think we need to. I feel like there's a snapping gator between us in the room every time we're together," he replied.

She took another sip from her cup and carefully set it back down on the table. "That night in New Orleans was completely out of character for me. I had recently lost my partner to a domestic altercation gone bad. I didn't want to be at the conference in the first place. I went to the bar to be alone and drown my grief in booze."

"And then I showed up."

For the first time since the day she'd arrived at the station in her official capacity, she smiled. The beauty, the memory of that smile punched him in the stomach.

"Yes, and then you showed up and you were charming and easy to talk to and suddenly you looked better than the booze." Her cheeks flamed a deeper pink. "It was a wild, crazy night that shouldn't have happened."

"Why did you use the name Lily?" he asked.

"My mother called me Lily from the time I was a little girl. Mom's name is Rose and she always told my father he had two beautiful flowers in the family. But it didn't take me long working in law enforcement to realize that people took me far more seriously as Olivia, which is my legal name. So I stopped being Lily and became Olivia and I named my daughter Lily."

"I have to admit I thought about you over the years. I wondered what had happened to you, if your career had taken off and if you'd found love."

Her eyes radiated surprise that was quickly masked. "It was only a month after that conference that I married and then got pregnant immediately. Phil was a great husband and father."

"Tell me more about him." Daniel said, wanting to know what kind of a man had captured her heart.

She leaned back in her chair and her features softened. An irrational stab of jealousy raced through Daniel. "Phil owned a small but successful restaurant. He had a huge heart and he loved me beyond reason. Even after my daughter, Lily, was born, he encouraged me to pursue my career. Along with my mother's help, we made a good team, me working law enforcement and him running his restaurant, and then he had a heart attack and died."

"Are you hoping to marry again?"

"I'm open to the possibility. I had a great husband and I know how good marriage can be, but if it doesn't happen I'm good alone with my mother helping me raise Lily and my career that consumes me."

"How old is your daughter?"

"She just turned four."

"I'm still attracted to you." The words fell from his mouth before his brain had fully formed them.

She cast her gaze away from him and out the nearby window where darkness had fallen. "I'm only here temporarily and I'm your boss. Any kind of a personal relationship between us would be completely out of line."

She looked at her wristwatch and then grabbed her purse. "Speaking of my mother and my daughter, I need to get home." She stood and looked toward the garage door. Daniel had a feeling she was escaping from the conversation rather than simply deciding it was time to go home.

Daniel got up to walk her to the door. "If it's any comfort, nobody knows about that night. I never mentioned it to anyone and have no intention of ever talking about it." He opened the door and punched the button inside to raise the garage door on the side where she had parked.

"I appreciate that. I'm here to do my job, Daniel, and nothing more." She stepped down the stairs to the garage floor and hurried to her car.

When she'd driven out and away, Daniel closed the door and returned to his chair at the table to finish his coffee. At least they'd talked about it, he thought.

However, she'd said nothing to tamp down a simmering desire that had grown inside him from the moment he'd seen her again.

More importantly, she'd told him all the reasons why they couldn't and shouldn't get involved again, but she hadn't said the one thing that would have shut him down permanently.

She hadn't said she wasn't attracted to him and in the omission of those words, he held on to just a little bit of hope that he would have her in his bed once again.

OLIVIA HAD A restless night. Both Lily and her mother had been asleep when she'd finally gotten in. She'd gone into Lily's room and kissed her sweet, sleeping daughter on the cheek and then had zapped a plate of leftover meat loaf that her mother had made for dinner.

By ten thirty she was on the futon, but sleep remained elusive as she played and replayed her conversation with Daniel in her head.

She hadn't wanted to talk about that night. She hadn't even wanted to think about it. She had spent far too many nights while married to Phil thinking about that single night of madness with Daniel.

Phil had been in love with her and she had loved Phil, but she hadn't been in love with him. He was a good, solid man and she'd been the best wife she could possibly be to him during their marriage. But it had been the one-night stand with Daniel that had haunted her dreams.

She was awakened the next morning to kisses being rained on her face and the scent of bacon filling the air. "Mommy, you didn't kiss me good-night last night and so you have to kiss me a zillion times this morning," Lily said. She was a vision of little-girl innocence in

her pink cotton nightgown and with her dark hair sleep tousled around her head.

"I think I can manage that," Olivia replied. She grabbed Lily and pulled her onto the futon with her and then proceeded to deliver kisses all over her daughter's face and neck.

Lily's giggles rang out, sweet music to Olivia's ears.

"Okay you two…breakfast in fifteen minutes," Rose said. "Lily, you can help me set the table while your mother gets ready for work."

Olivia took a fast shower, dressed in a pair of tailored black slacks and a white blouse and then joined her mother and daughter at the table for bacon and pancakes.

Breakfast was always a joy when the three of them shared it together. Rose had been a loving, nurturing mother to Olivia and once Lily was born, she'd become beloved Nanny and had watched Lily whenever Olivia and Phil were at work.

Rose was a wonderful mix of common sense and naïveté. She had a good sense of humor and a fierce love of her little family. She believed the world was a good and happy place, and Olivia never brought the evil she worked with home to share with her mother.

Many times over the years Olivia had downplayed the danger she'd faced at work in an effort to protect her mother from worry.

"As usual, a great breakfast, Mom," Olivia said.

"It's always good if it's got syrup," Lily quipped and

used her tongue to capture an errant dollop of the sweet goo that had escaped onto her lower lip.

"Are you going to be late tonight?" Rose asked.

"You'd better be here to kiss me good-night," Lily exclaimed.

"I kissed you while you were sleeping last night. Besides, you know how it works. If I'm not here to kiss you good-night, then Nanny gives you double kisses," Olivia replied.

"And I think I gave her triple kisses last night," Rose exclaimed.

Minutes later Olivia left the house and headed for the station. She hoped the issue of her and Daniel's previous encounter had been laid to rest, for she was depending on him to accompany her as she interviewed some of the key players in the two-year-old murder case of Shelly Sinclair.

So he'd thought about her over the years. His words had surprised her. She'd always figured she'd been nothing more than a slight blip on his radar. A sexy guy like him had to have had plenty of hookups before and after that night they'd shared.

Of course it didn't matter if he'd thought about her or her about him. It didn't matter if he was still attracted to her and she was attracted to him. Nothing would ever come of it.

She wasn't a young, vulnerable woman anymore. In fact, she rarely thought of herself as a woman. She was a mother, but she was also a law enforcement of-

ficial. She wore those titles much more easily than that of simply a woman.

It was nine o'clock when she and Daniel left the station and got into her car to drive to Claire Silver's small house on the swamp side of town where she lived with her new husband, Bo.

"Bo moved in with Claire when his family home was burned down by the high school coach who had become Claire's frightening stalker. They got married a couple of weeks ago," Daniel said.

"I read the file on Claire's stalker, Roger Cantor," Olivia replied. She'd been grateful that there was no awkwardness between her and Daniel. It was as if their conversation the night before had never happened, and that was the way she wanted it. In fact, the tension between them that had been apparent since they'd first seen each other had dissipated.

Daniel guided her to a renovated shanty much like where Olivia was staying. "They're my neighbors," she said as she pulled her car to a halt in front of the house. "I'm staying five houses down in the bright yellow place."

Daniel had called ahead to let Bo and Claire know they were coming, and Bo opened the door before they reached it. "Daniel," he said in greeting and then held out a hand to Olivia. "Sheriff Bradford, it's nice to meet you."

Bo McBride had a firm handshake and clear blue eyes that appeared as if they wouldn't know how to hide a secret. His dark hair was long and slightly shaggy and his features were well-defined and handsome. "Please, come in," he said and gestured them into a small living room where a petite curly-haired blonde woman stood at their appearance.

Further introductions were made and then the four of them sat at the kitchen table where Claire offered them something to drink and they declined.

"I'm glad you're reopening the case into Shelly's murder," Bo said.

"News travels fast around here," Olivia replied drily.

"The small town gossip mill is alive and well," Bo replied and then frowned. "I was basically run out of town on a rail in the weeks after her death because of nothing but gossip. Sheriff Walker made it clear that I was guilty and it was only because they couldn't find evidence that I was still walking around free. It destroyed the life I'd had here."

Claire placed a hand on Bo's arm. "Bo couldn't kill anyone, especially not Shelly, who he loved with all his heart."

Olivia pulled out a small pad and pen from her purse. "I need you to tell me everything you can about that time. I want names of the people Shelly was close to, ideas you might have as to who might have wanted her dead…anything that will guide us as we dig into this case."

For the next hour, Bo talked about his long-term relationship with Shelly. He was honest about the fact that he wasn't sure if Shelly ever would have married him, that she had longed for a life away from Lost Lagoon.

But, Bo's successful business was here, along with his mother, and he had no desire to leave the small town.

Both Olivia and Daniel asked questions and not once did Olivia get the feeling that Bo was hiding anything from them. He confessed to them that he still owned Jimmy's Place, that at the time of the murder many of his customers had turned away and that was when he suggested to his best friend, Jimmy Tambor, that he take over as manager and rename the place.

For almost two years following Shelly's murder, Bo had built a new life for himself in Jackson, coming back to Lost Lagoon only in the dead of night on the weekends to visit his mother, whose house Jimmy had moved into to help care take of her.

"I came back a couple of months ago when my mother passed away and while I was here I met Claire." He covered her petite hand with his and smiled at her lovingly. "She convinced me to stay in town and fight for my innocence, but then her life was in danger and my sole concern became keeping her safe."

"So, you haven't done much investigating on your own into Shelly's murder," Olivia said.

"If you're asking me if I know who killed Shelly, then the answer is no. I'm no closer to knowing today than I was on the night she was murdered," he replied. "All I know is I didn't do it and I'm as eager as anyone to get the killer arrested." His eyes blazed fervently.

"So, what did you think?" Daniel asked Olivia once they were back in her car.

"I'm mostly a facts-only kind of person, but my gut instinct says that he's being truthful," she replied.

"How about we grab a hamburger at George's Diner before we head back to the station?" he suggested. "It's not too far down the road from here."

Olivia glanced at her watch. It was just after eleven. "All right," she agreed. She'd eat a quick lunch and be back in her office by noon to check in on things there and to write up a complete report on the interview with Bo and Claire.

Daniel pointed the way, and before long she was parked in front of the small building with a huge sign on top that read George's Diner.

"It doesn't look big enough to be a diner," she said as they got out of the car.

"I told you it's really just a glorified hamburger joint. Most people order and take out. There are only five stools at a counter inside. George has everything from fried gator to shrimp scampi on his menu, but most people come here for the burgers. It's a dive but he makes the best burgers you'll ever wrap your mouth around."

The interior of the small establishment was empty and held the gamy odor of the swamp and hot grease. "We'll eat in the car," Olivia whispered, finding the variety of cooking smells unpleasant.

At that moment a big man lumbered out of what she assumed was the kitchen. Jowls bounced as he greeted them with a smile and slapped two menus in front of them.

"I heard there was a new sheriff in town." His deep

voice resembled that of a croaking bullfrog. "George King," he said. He swiped a hand on his dirty white apron and held it across the counter to her.

Olivia shook his hand and mentally thought of the small bottle of hand sanitizer she kept in her purse. "Sheriff Bradford," she replied as she shook his thick, meaty hand.

"So, what can I get for you two? I got some fresh gator meat in this morning," George said.

"No gator," Daniel replied. "We'll take two of your special burgers and a couple of sodas to go."

"Got it." George disappeared back into the kitchen area.

"Did he know Shelly?" Olivia asked.

Daniel smiled. "Everyone knew Shelly. Why?"

"George is a big man with big hands. It would have been easy for him to strangle a young woman and then toss her into the lagoon."

Daniel's grin widened. "Once a lawman, always a lawman."

"Exactly," she replied, wishing his smile didn't create a ball of heat in the pit of her stomach.

Minutes later they were back in her car. She used her hand sanitizer, placed a couple of napkins on her lap and then took the gigantic burger wrapped in foil from Daniel. Daniel, too, had placed a napkin across his lap.

Two beef patties, two kinds of cheeses, tomato and lettuce, bacon and barbecue sauce, the first bite created an explosion of flavor in her mouth.

"Tell the truth, it's the best you've ever tasted," Daniel said with a knowing smile.

She finished chewing and swallowed. "Okay, I admit it."

They ate in silence and when they were finished, Daniel took their trash to a nearby bin and disposed of it and then they were back on the road headed back to the station.

"Still listen to blues music?" he asked.

It had been part of their conversation at the bar, the fact that they both loved old blues classics. "These days my music list mostly exists of 'Itsy Bitsy Spider,' 'The Wheels on the Bus' and any songs from kids' shows. What about you?"

"Still love my Billie Holiday and of course B.B. King," he replied.

They spent the rest of the ride talking about the old masters of blues music. Once they returned to the station, Olivia headed to her office and Daniel returned to his desk.

It sat in the middle of her desk, a brown-wrapped package addressed to her. It didn't belong there and she had no idea how it had gotten there.

She opened her office door and saw Daniel and Josh talking together. "Josh… Daniel, could you come in here?" She hoped her voice didn't betray a faint whisper of fear the presence of the unexpected package had wrought inside her.

Both men got up and when they entered her office she pointed to a brown-wrapped box on her desk.

"That was here when I came in. I didn't touch it, but it doesn't have any postage and it's addressed to me."

Daniel frowned in obvious concern. "How did it get here?"

"I don't know. It was just here," she replied.

"I'll go get Betsy," Josh said. He left the office. Betsy Rogers was the dispatcher/receptionist.

"You weren't expecting any deliveries of any kind?" Daniel asked.

She gave a curt shake of her head. "No, nothing."

"I'll grab my fingerprint kit," Daniel said.

By the time he returned to the office, Josh and Betsy were also there. "It was left just outside of the front entrance," Betsy said. "I don't know how long it was there. Ray noticed it when he came back from lunch and gave it to me and I brought it in here."

"Then you didn't see who left it or how it was delivered?" Josh asked.

"I don't even know how long it was out there," Betsy replied.

Daniel pulled on a pair of gloves and approached the box. It looked fairly benign other than the fact that there was no return mailing address or official mail markings.

Josh and Olivia stood in the office doorway. Was it a bomb? Had she already made enemies she didn't know about? Or maybe it was a welcoming gift from somebody in town. She didn't want to jump to conclusions, but she definitely didn't like surprises.

"It's light," Daniel said. "I don't think it's a bomb or anything like that."

He opened his fingerprinting kit and got to work. Olivia watched as he carefully brushed the top of the box. "Got one here," he said and transferred the print to a piece of tape and then placed it on a card where he wrote where it had been found.

It was a tedious process and Olivia found herself holding her breath. She wanted any fingerprints from the package, but more important, she wanted to know what was inside.

Although it could be something nice, like home-baked cookies or a handmade knickknack with a note inside saying who it was from, she still couldn't shake a bad feeling.

It took nearly twenty minutes for Daniel to finish fingerprinting the entire package. He pulled two different sets of prints from it. "I imagine the prints belong to Ray and Betsy. Their prints are on file so I can easily compare them," he said.

"But the fact that you found no other prints means whoever left it probably wore gloves," Josh said, his words only increasing Olivia's nervous tension. "Open it."

"I'll open it," Olivia said. If there was anything inside that might be harmful, then it was her job to shield her deputies.

Daniel looked as if he wanted to argue with her, but she gave him a stern look and he stepped aside. She tried to keep her fingers from trembling as she carefully removed the brown outer wrapping to reveal a plain white box with a fitted lid.

She removed the lid and sighed in relief as nothing exploded or shot out. Inside was a wad of tissue paper. She pulled it out and stared at the contents, her brain momentarily unable to make sense of it.

A stuffed dark brown dog was in the bottom, its throat slashed and white stuffing spilling out. A folded piece of paper was nestled next to the mutilated toy.

"Let me," Daniel said tersely. He still wore his gloves and he plucked the paper from the box and opened it. In bright red lettering it read: Let Sleeping Dogs Lie.

"I think we can assume from this that Shelly's killer is still here in town," Josh finally said.

"And reopening the case has him shaken up," Daniel added.

Olivia stared down at the note and then at the ripped little dog. She tried, without success, to stop the icy chill that crept up her spine.

Chapter Four

Daniel was ticked off and worried. He'd hated to see the fear that had momentarily filled Olivia's eyes. He also hated the fact that somebody was warning them off the case, for the package contents could only be taken as a warning.

Somebody had moved damn fast, since they'd only officially reopened Shelly's case the day before.

He'd moved the package into the evidence room and Olivia had insisted she was fine and needed to write reports. He'd left her alone in her office and spent the next couple of hours checking out the fingerprints he'd pulled. Just as he suspected, they'd matched both Ray and Betsy.

He'd also talked to Ray, who had spent his lunch hour at the Lost Lagoon Café and had spied the package against the building near the front door when he'd returned.

Part of the problem was that he doesn't know how seriously to take the warning. Was it a direct threat against Olivia? Or was it just some fool thinking it would be funny to shake up the new sheriff?

He definitely intended to err on the side of caution. Apparently, Olivia was on the same page. It was almost four in the afternoon when she called him into her office.

"You doing okay?" he asked as he closed the door behind him.

Her eyes were dark, but her features were more relaxed than they had been before. "I'm fine, but I'm not sure if I should be. I'm not particularly concerned about my own safety, but I am a little worried for my mother and Lily."

"Why don't I follow you to your place after work and I can check things out there for you?" The last thing he wanted was for her to worry about her family.

"Oh, that's not necessary," she protested with a vehemence that wasn't warranted by the situation.

"Humor me," he replied. "I'd feel better if I took a look around."

She didn't appear particularly pleased, but she finally nodded her head. "Okay, I should be leaving here in about an hour."

"I'll be ready," he said and then once again left her alone in the office.

"You worried?" Josh asked as he scooted his chair closer to Daniel's.

"I'm concerned. I don't know whether to be really worried or not," Daniel admitted.

"It could have been just some sort of sick prank," Josh said, but his tone of voice indicated he didn't believe his own words.

"Maybe, but just to be on the safe side I'm heading over to Olivia's place after work to check out the locks she has on her doors and windows. She's not so afraid for herself, but she's concerned about her mother and daughter being safe."

"She has a mother and a kid?" Josh looked at Daniel in surprise. "I figured she was hatched from a bad-ass badge and I definitely didn't figure her for the maternal type."

Daniel smiled inwardly. Although Olivia had only shown herself to be tough and strictly professional while in this building and in Lost Lagoon, he had memories of a much softer, much hotter Olivia in his mind.

"She wasn't hatched and she does have a mother and a little girl here with her," Daniel said.

"Divorced?"

"Widowed," Daniel replied.

"I'm sure she wore the pants in that family," Ray quipped from his desk.

Daniel looked at him with irritation. "Don't you have something better to do than eavesdrop on private conversations?"

"As a matter of fact, I do." Ray got up from his desk. "I'm outta here. I'm meeting a couple of buddies at Jimmy's Place for a few drinks."

"I'd eat my hat if that man ever stayed to the end of his shift," Josh said drily once Ray had left the squad room. "You think he's dirty?"

"Hard to tell." Daniel reared back in his chair. "He was definitely close to Walker, but it's possible Ray really didn't know about the drug trafficking. I mean, let's be honest here—Ray isn't the brightest color in the box, and Trey probably didn't trust him to keep their dirty little secret. If he is dirty, Sheriff Bradford will figure it out."

"Anyone else she looking at closely?" Josh asked.

"Maybe Fowler," Daniel replied, knowing he could trust his friend not to take the information any further. "And that's just between the two of us," he added anyway.

"Randy definitely came into some money from somewhere."

"If there's any dirt in the department, the sheriff will sweep it out. That's what she's here for, but she definitely wants to close out Shelly's case, as well."

"That ripped-up dog was creepy. I hope it was somebody's idea of a sick joke."

A knot of tension formed in Daniel's chest. "Yeah, so do I."

The men got back to work and twenty minutes later, Olivia appeared in the office doorway. "I'm ready to head home."

Daniel stood and together they left the building by the back door and stepped out into the parking area. Olivia always drove her private car to work, but used her official patrol car during the day.

She now headed to her private car, a four-door navy sedan with a child's car seat buckled into the backseat. "I'm sure this isn't necessary," she said. "There are locks on the doors and windows. I just panicked for a minute when I saw that dog and the note."

"Panic isn't a bad thing," he replied easily. "I'd just like to check things out to assure myself that your family is safe and sound when you aren't home."

He realized he didn't intend to take no for an answer. Not only did he want to check the security of the house, he wanted to meet her mother and daughter, see Olivia in the setting of her home and family.

"Knock yourself out," she finally said. She got into her car and Daniel hurried toward his.

Minutes later he pulled up in front of the small bright yellow place where Olivia was living during her time in Lost Lagoon. He jumped out of his car and caught up with her on the front porch.

They scarcely cleared the door when she was attacked by a little dark-haired girl who threw herself at Olivia. Olivia crouched down and grabbed her daughter close, her features soft and loving as she nuzzled little Lily's neck. Her laughter mingled with Lily's.

This was a side to Sheriff Bradford that none of the other men would see—the soft, maternal side that Daniel was surprised to discover he found crazy attractive.

A woman, presumably Olivia's mother, stood at the stove and smiled at Daniel. She was an attractive woman with dark hair and eyes like Olivia's. "Just give them a minute and then we'll introduce ourselves," she said loud enough to be heard over the giggles.

Olivia released her daughter and stood. "Mom, this

is Deputy Carson, and this is my mother, Rose. And this little munchkin is Lily."

"Hey Deputy, you want to see my room?" Lily asked, her green eyes bright with friendliness.

"Maybe in a little while," Olivia replied. "Right now Deputy Carson is going to check out the doors and windows in the house."

Rose's expression turned to one of simmering panic. "Has something happened? Is something wrong?"

"Not at all," Daniel replied smoothly. "Whenever somebody moves into one of these renovated shanties, somebody from the sheriff's department does a sort of well check on the place. You'd be surprised how sloppy and cheap some people are when they renovate."

"How nice," Rose said. She relaxed and Olivia smiled at him gratefully. Her smile, so rare and so beautiful, filled him with warmth.

"I'm just finishing up a big pot of jambalaya and a pan of corn bread," Rose said. "After you do your check, you'll eat with us." Daniel started to protest, but Rose raised a hand to stop him. "It's no extra work and I insist."

"You can put honey on your corn bread, Deputy, and it's really, really good," Lily said.

Daniel smiled at the cute child who looked so much like her mother. "How can I turn down corn bread with honey? And why don't you show me your room? I'd love to see it."

Lily nodded eagerly and grabbed his hand. A new, different kind of warmth swept through him at the feel of her tiny hand grasping his. "Come on," she said. "It's mostly pink."

It was definitely pink—pink bedspread and pink curtains at the window. Lily showed him her princess shoes and her fashion dollhouse. Olivia stood in the doorway, her smile one of bemusement as Lily insisted he sit on her twin bed to see how comfy it was.

Lily was chatty and cute and obviously bright as she continued to give him a tour of everything in the room. He finally walked over to the window and opened it. He then closed it, turned the lock and tried to open it again. It didn't budge.

"Why did you do that?" Lily asked.

"Uh, to make sure when it rains it can't rain inside," he replied. "And now I need to check all the windows in all the rooms."

"I'll help you, Deputy," Lily said eagerly.

Olivia shadowed them as they went into Rose's room where a double bed was neatly made up with a yellow-flowered spread and white gauzy curtains were opened to allow in the late afternoon sunshine.

"Nanny won't get wet," Lily said once they'd tested her window. "If the window let in rain she could always wear a raincoat to sleep in, but that would be silly."

"That would be silly, but now we know she won't have to do that," Daniel replied.

With Lily's help they finished checking every window in the house. All of them locked firmly and the only issue Daniel saw was the locks on the doors.

"You need dead bolts on the doors," Daniel said once

they were all back in the small living room and standing in front of the black futon where he realized Olivia must spend her nights. "I'll head out now to the hardware store and grab a couple and install them."

"Oh, no, I can't let you do that," Olivia protested.

He smiled at her. "You can't stop me from doing that," he replied.

"By the time you get back, supper will be ready to serve and I'm not letting you get out of here without eating a good meal for all of your trouble," Rose said.

Daniel left the house and got back into his car. Although he'd wanted to check the general safety of the house, he was almost sorry he'd come.

Seeing Olivia interact with her mother and daughter had shown him a new dimension to her. He admired and respected Sheriff Olivia Bradford. He'd once lusted over a woman named Lily. But seeing Olivia soft and maternal had reignited a desire for her that wasn't just based in lust.

It was confusing, and he'd never been confused about a woman before in his life.

"He seems like a nice man," Rose said and checked the pan of corn bread in the oven.

"I like Deputy," Lily said. "I think you should marry him and let him be my daddy."

"Honey, his name isn't Deputy. You should call him Mr. Carson," Olivia replied.

Lily shook her head and raised her chin with a hint

of stubbornness. "I like Deputy and he likes me to call him that, too."

Olivia decided it wasn't worth arguing about. "Okay, but I'm not marrying Deputy and he isn't father material."

"He still seems like a nice young man," Rose said.

"He is," Olivia agreed.

"And what a nice thing for the department to do, a sort of well check on these shanties to make sure they're all safe," Rose said.

It was Rose's naïveté that allowed her to even believe such a thing. "I'm going to change clothes," Olivia said, eager to get out of her work clothing and into something more comfortable.

She went into her mother's room where her clothes were stored in drawers and hanging in the closet along with Rose's, but instead of immediately grabbing something to change into she sank down on the edge of the bed and drew a deep breath.

Seeing Daniel with Lily had twisted her heart in ways it had never been twisted before. He'd been so easy, so natural with her. Many nights she had dreamed of what it might be like if the two of them ever met, if they ever knew each other.

But he was a confirmed bachelor and had no desire for children. Nothing could be served by telling him the truth about Lily now. And oddly that broke her heart more than just a little bit.

Lily would never know about her real father. When she got old enough to ask questions, Olivia would tell her about Phil Bradford and how much he had loved his family, how much he had adored Lily.

She got up from the bed and grabbed a pair of denim shorts and a chocolate-colored T-shirt. While she dressed, she thought of that moment when Lily had said that she wanted Olivia to marry "Deputy" and he'd become her daddy.

Olivia had worked with plenty of men in the past, men who Lily had met and spent time with, but she'd never indicated that she was interested in any of them becoming her daddy.

Was it some sort of nebulous blood tie that had made Lily take so easily to Daniel? In the year since Phil had died, she'd occasionally thought about the possibility of remarrying eventually. In an ideal world, she would like Lily to have a strong male presence in her life as she grew up.

But that man wasn't Daniel. And despite the desire she had for a repeat of what they had shared in New Orleans, he would never be her husband and Lily's father.

She dressed and then went into the bathroom and removed the clasp from the back of her neck, allowing her hair to flow free beyond her shoulders. She breathed a sigh of relief as she brushed the long strands. By the end of the day she always had a tiny headache from having her hair so tightly bound.

By the time she left the bathroom, Daniel had returned, sporting two dead bolts, one for each door. They were simple but sturdy slide locks that mounted to the door and frame. He'd brought with him the tools he needed and set to work with Lily watching him and keeping up a running conversation.

Olivia set the table for four while Rose pulled the corn bread from the oven. Within twenty minutes they were all seated at the table with bowls of the southern stew in front of them and big slabs of corn bread sliced and served.

Lily grabbed the bottle of honey and looked at Daniel. "You have to drizzle it, not glob it. That's the best way," she instructed. She drizzled her piece of corn bread and then handed the honey bottle to Daniel. "Now you drizzle, Deputy."

Daniel grinned at Olivia and did as Lily had told him. The scene was so domestic and shot a pang of longing through Olivia. She steeled herself against the warm, fuzzy feeling. This was a moment of fantasy and had nothing to do with reality.

Daniel not only charmed Lily, but Rose, as well, praising her for the tasty food and talking to her about the garden she had back in Natchez. He even encouraged her to share stories about Olivia's childhood, which made Daniel and Lily laugh and Olivia cringe.

She was both slightly disappointed and equally relieved when the meal was finished, and Daniel was ready to leave after insisting he help with the cleanup.

"Thank you for the best meal I've had in months," he said to Rose and then crouched down in front of Lily. "And thank you for showing me your room and especially your princess shoes. They were beautiful."

Lily grabbed him around the neck and then kissed

him on the cheek. Olivia didn't know who was more stunned, her or Daniel. "We like you, Deputy. We hope you come back again," Lily said as she released him.

Daniel straightened up, a stunned expression still on his face. The expression slowly faded and he looked at Rose. "Now that I've installed those dead bolts, you need to use them anytime you and Lily are here alone. This area sometimes has some drunks wandering around." He looked back at Olivia. "Walk me out?"

She nodded and after final goodbyes, she followed him to his car parked along the side of the street. "You have a charming family," he said as they reached his car.

"Thanks, I'm pretty partial to them," she replied.

He frowned. "Olivia, those dead bolts I put on your doors are only temporary stop locks. If somebody really wanted into your house badly enough they could use enough force to get through those locks. I recommend you contact Buck Ranier. He owns a personal security company and could guarantee you a safer environment here."

"I don't want to overreact to what's happened," she replied. "So far all we have is an anonymous warning that I'm assuming is because of reopening the Sinclair case."

"I certainly don't want to scare you, but I also don't want to underreact to that package you got today," he replied, his eyes the deep green of the dark swamp.

"I appreciate you putting in the dead bolts, but I'm not ready to have a full alarm system installed. I don't want to frighten my mother if it isn't absolutely necessary. I just want to get more information about the package and who might have sent it and definitely why. We don't know for sure that it had anything to do with reopening the Sinclair case."

"I'd say it's a good guess that it's concerning the Sinclair case. Besides, we might not get any more information about the package," he replied. "We asked around. Nobody saw it placed where it was found. We've got no fingerprints or postage stamp to work with."

He broke off and reached out and touched a strand of her hair that had fallen forward over her shoulder. "I just don't want to see anything bad happen to you or your family." He grimaced and dropped his hand to his side and stepped back from her. "I'll see you in the morning," he said curtly.

She stood and watched him get into his car and remained watching until the vehicle was out of her sight. That simple, yet inappropriate touch to her hair had stirred her as had his obvious concern for their safety.

She turned to walk back to the house. Daniel had been a deputy here in Lost Lagoon for a long time and he was worried about her and her family. Was she underplaying the danger to herself...to her family?

It had just been a stupid stuffed animal and a note, the act of a coward, she told herself. She wished this assignment was over already.

She wished Shelly's murder was solved and she'd rooted out any dirty officers who might still be working in the department. As much as anything, she wished she hadn't seen Daniel and Lily together.

At least he hadn't asked too many questions about her quick marriage and pregnancy. It obviously hadn't entered his mind that he could possibly be Lily's father.

Still, she now felt threatened not just on a physical level, but on an emotional one, as well.

Chapter Five

"How about lunch at Jimmy's Place?" Daniel asked Olivia the next day at noon. He knew that Olivia had spent the morning combing through old files, looking for errors and checking evidence reports on Walker's reports.

Daniel had been in the small room that the task force had been assigned to work out of for the Sinclair case. If the note and the stuffed animal were, indeed, about this case, then he had a renewed determination to get it solved as quickly as possible.

"That man should have been shot," Olivia said minutes later when she was in the passenger side of Daniel's car and they were headed to Jimmy's Place down the street.

"I'm assuming you're talking about Walker," he replied.

"His files are a mess with half-written or missing reports." She drew in a deep breath as if to neutralize her irritation. "Anything new with the task force?"

"Nothing. Derrick and Wes have interviewed all of Shelly's girlfriends at the time of her murder, but nothing new has come up. Josh has been asking around to see if anyone saw somebody leave the package in front of the building. I suggested Jimmy's Place for lunch because I think it's important that you be seen around town and it's possible we'll run into some suspects there."

"And it will show the creep who sent me that stuffed dog that I'm not backing off." Her voice was firm and strong. There was no hint of the soft woman he'd seen the night before at her place. If he thought about it too long, his fingers would tingle with the memory of her silky hair from his brief touch of it the night before.

He found an empty parking space around the back of the building and together they got out and walked around to the front door.

Jimmy Tambor, Bo's best friend, greeted them. "Sheriff Bradford, it's good to finally meet you in person," he said. "Bo has told me he has a lot of faith that you'll finally be able to put Shelly's case to rest."

"That's the plan," Olivia replied.

"As you can see, we've got a pretty full house, but I've got either a table or a booth still open," Jimmy said as he grabbed two menus off a small hostess table.

"A booth would be good," Daniel said. He much preferred the intimacy of a booth.

"Just follow me." Jimmy led them to an empty booth midway down one wall. He had no sooner moved away when Daniel saw acting mayor Frank Kean, city councilman Neil Sampson and amusement park owner Rod Nixon making their way toward them.

"Incoming," he said to Olivia, who straightened in the seat.

"Sheriff, good to see you," Frank said as the three men stood by the booth. "I wanted to introduce you to two important men in town. City councilman Neil Sampson has been my right-hand man since I was thrust back into office, and Rod Nixon owns the amusement park being built on the ridge."

Olivia greeted each of them and a bit of small talk ensued. "So, how are things coming in the Sinclair case?" Neil asked. "Are you going to catch the bad guy?"

"That's what we all want," Olivia replied.

"Hopefully long before the amusement park opens," Rod said. "We're highlighting a pirate theme, but we wouldn't want people coming here to hear about an unsolved murder case of a young woman."

"We're hoping to capitalize on the underground tunnels in coordination with the amusement park," Neil said. "Paid tours through pirate paths…of course, we'll add some special effects to make it more exciting for the tourists. But, we all want Shelly's case solved. It's been unresolved for too long."

"We're pursuing several leads," Daniel said curtly. The waitress appeared at the booth. "And now if you'll excuse us, we're about to order lunch."

The men moved away and Olivia and Daniel placed their orders with the waitress, then Olivia eyed Daniel with speculation. "Okay, tell me who of those three men you don't like."

He looked at her in surprise. "What? Can you read my mind now?"

She smiled. "I'm beginning to identify your tones and facial expressions."

"That's a little bit scary," he replied with a small laugh and then sobered. "I'm not a big fan of Neil Sampson. He's ambitious to a fault and arrogant and thinks he's God's gift to all females."

"He is a nice-looking man," Olivia said.

"He's a pompous ass," Daniel returned, surprised by the twinge of jealousy that rose up inside him by her words.

They stopped talking as the waitress appeared with their orders. Olivia had ordered mozzarella sticks and a Cobb salad while Daniel had opted for a meatball sandwich and seasoned fries.

"Hmm, I'm going to have to order some of these to take home some evening for Lily," Olivia said after taking a bite of one of the cheese sticks. "Lily would eat mozzarella sticks for every meal if I'd let her."

"She's quite a little charmer, and your mother is also very nice. I enjoyed meeting them both."

"They enjoyed meeting you, too." She grabbed another mozzarella stick. "And now, let's talk about who we need to interview next in an effort to solve Shelly's murder."

The last thing Olivia wanted to talk about was Daniel's visit the night before. Lily had chattered about "Deputy" until she'd fallen asleep, and even Rose had been quite taken with Daniel.

Olivia didn't want him spending any more time with her family. She didn't want to see father and daughter together. The sight of them interacting created a deep ache in her heart that would never be eased.

"I think the next person we should interview is Eric Baptiste. He apparently had developed a friendship with Shelly just before her death. If Shelly wanted a ticket out of town, Eric would have been a good bet. He's got a degree in botany and could probably get a job teaching at some college anywhere."

"And we still need to talk with Mac Sinclair. It's hard to believe a brother might kill a sister, but we both know anything is possible when it comes to murder," Olivia replied.

"Savannah mentioned to Josh that she's secretly been afraid that Mac might be responsible. Apparently, Mac hated Bo and didn't want Shelly with him. Savannah wonders if maybe Mac met Shelly that night and they argued about Bo, and if things got heated and in a rage Mac strangled Shelly."

Olivia took a bite of her salad and considered the theory. "That might explain the missing engagement ring. Even in death he removed the one thing that tied her to Bo."

"Makes a horrible kind of sense," Daniel said. He took a huge bite of his sandwich and washed it down with a gulp of sweet tea. "So, who do you want to talk to after lunch? Eric would probably be the easiest because he should be working at the apothecary shop."

"Then Eric it is," she agreed. "We can plan on talking to Mac tomorrow."

"Sounds like a plan."

They fell silent as they continued with their lunch. Olivia found herself gazing around at the patrons, wondering if a murderer was dining here right now.

They had a handful of suspects, but no real evidence to even know if any one of their suspects should be on a short list. Supposition and conjecture, that's all they had at the moment and it was definitely frustrating.

It's only been a couple of days, she reminded herself. She shouldn't expect results so quickly. She glanced at Daniel, who was also dividing his attention between his food and the other diners.

Every time she looked at him, a memory of the passionate night they'd shared exploded in her head and a ball of simmering desire to repeat that night burned in the pit of her stomach and that was as frustrating as the unsolved crime.

After they ate, they drove down the street to Mama Baptiste's Apothecary and Gift Shop. The minute they entered, Oliva's nose filled with the scent of mysterious herbs and her attention was captured by the plants and strange-looking roots that hung from the ceiling.

Mama Baptiste was a large woman with long dark hair shot through with shiny silver strands. Clad in a bright pink peasant-style blouse and a swirling long floral skirt, she looked free-spirited.

She greeted them with a bright smile, and Daniel made the introductions between the two women. "You know he's one of my favorite deputies," Mama said and grinned.

"She says that about all of us," Daniel replied in a teasing tone. "I'll bet I won't be one of your favorites when you know why we're here. We need to talk to Eric."

Mama's smile immediately fell. "What's this about?" She looked at Olivia. "Every time anything goes wrong in this town, my boy is the first one looked at. It isn't fair. He minds his own business and doesn't look for trouble."

"We're just trying to tie up some loose ends," Olivia said.

Mama heaved a deep sigh and pointed toward the back of the store. "He's in the storeroom."

When they walked toward the back, Olivia saw that Mama didn't just sell whatever concoctions she made from her roots and herbs, but the store also held silly voodoo kits and a variety of crystals and some pirate hats and plastic swords obviously intended for tourists.

Eric Baptiste was a dark-haired, dark-eyed man around thirty. Attractive in a bad-boy, mysterious kind of way, he winced at the sight of them. "What now?" he asked.

"I'm Sheriff Bradford," Olivia said. "I'm sure you've heard that we've reopened the case of Shelly Sinclair's death, and we'd like to do a follow-up interview with you."

Eric raked a hand through his thick, shaggy hair. "Does this mean I need to come down to the station with you?"

on't see any reason why we can't just talk here,"
i replied. She knew from experience that it was
r to get information from somebody who was com-
able in their own surroundings.

Eric shrugged. "Whatever." He grabbed two folding chairs leaning against the wall and opened them,
then sat on the top of a large box and gestured her and
Daniel to the chairs.

Olivia sat and pulled out her pad and pen from her
purse. Daniel also sat and leaned back against the wall,
as if content to let her conduct the interview. That was
fine with her. She had no preconceived impressions
where Eric was concerned.

"I've read the notes from when you were previously
interviewed following Shelly's murder. I understand
that at the time of her murder you were in your house
alone and nobody could substantiate your whereabouts."

Eric's eyes narrowed. "If I'd known that night that
Shelly was going to be killed and I'd need an alibi, I
would have made sure to have somebody in my bed
with me."

Olivia straightened in the chair, not liking the sar-
castic tone of his voice. "It's come to light recently that
you and Shelly had become quite friendly before her
death," she said. She studied Eric intently and saw a
brief wash of grief sweep over his features. It was there
only a moment and then gone.

"We'd gotten friendly," he admitted. "Sometimes at
night when she was working at The Pirate's Inn, I'd visit

her to pass some of the night. It wasn't anything romantic or anything like that. We were friends, that's all."

"She never talked to you about the two of you skipping town and heading for big city lights?"

"She talked about moving to a big city, but it was just talk and it never included me. I have no desire to leave Lost Lagoon. My mother is here alone and she isn't getting any younger."

His eyes softened and any sarcasm he might have had before was gone. "I don't have many friends and I enjoyed Shelly's company on occasion. I would never hurt her. I definitely had no reason to kill her."

"Did Shelly know about the tunnels underground?" Daniel asked.

"Not that I know of. I think she would have mentioned them to me if she had known about them."

"Do you have any idea who murdered Shelly?" Olivia asked.

Eric shook his head and his eyes once again went flat and dark. "No, but I wish I did. There's very little kindness in this town, and Shelly was kind and good." He stood. "And now if we're finished here, I've got work to do."

Olivia and Daniel also stood. "Thank you for your time, Eric," Olivia said. "Please let me know if you think of anything that might help in the investigation."

Eric cast her a rueful smile. "I've had two years to think about it. If I knew anything worthwhile I would have already told somebody. She deserves justice."

Olivia asked another handful of questions, but got nothing of substance.

"What do you think?" Daniel asked when they were back in the car and headed down the street to the station.

"I'm not sure," she replied. "I think it's possible he's telling the truth, but I also believe it's equally possible that he and Shelly might have stepped over the line of friendship. He seemed pretty intense about her."

"Shelly mentioned to several of her friends that she had a sticky situation on her hands, but didn't go into any detail with anyone. Maybe the sticky situation was that she found herself in love with two men, Bo and Eric."

"Even if that's the case, we still aren't any closer to knowing who killed Shelly. Eric didn't seem inclined to admit if his friendship with Shelly had developed into something more." She was aware of the frustration in her voice.

"We'll figure it out," Daniel replied, his voice soft, yet filled with determination.

The skies had begun to darken with thick clouds, portending the early evening rainstorm the forecasters had predicted that morning. The dark clouds mirrored Olivia's mood.

She'd hoped Eric would visibly show signs of lying, that he'd slip up and say something self-incriminating, but that hadn't happened.

Now she'd spend the rest of the afternoon working on the internal investigation of the officers in the department, and Daniel and the rest of the small task force would convene to talk about how little they had learned so far.

Once she was in her private office, she found concentration difficult. She could only hope that in Shelly's case things would become clearer after they'd interviewed several more people.

It didn't help that she was spending so much time with Daniel. His very nearness enticed her to throw caution to the wind, to jump into bed with him. She knew he'd be more than willing, that he desired her. She'd seen it in his gazes, felt it like a simmering cauldron between them.

But the last thing she needed was another one-night stand with a man who had no interest in a real relationship. Besides, doing something so foolish would only undermine her authority here.

With grim determination she pulled out several files of the men who worked for her in her search for somebody who had abused their position and potentially committed criminal acts.

It was just after six when she finally pulled her head from her work and glanced out the window, shocked to see that the black clouds had created an early, false night-like semidarkness.

She put away the files and grabbed her purse, hoping to get home before the clouds released a deluge of rain. Daniel was at his desk when she stepped out of the office.

"Calling it a day?" he asked.

"I want to stop by Jimmy's Place and get an order of

mozzarella sticks for Lily and then hopefully get home before the rain starts."

"I'm heading out pretty quickly, too," he replied. "Other than Josh, most of the other day-shift people went home a little while ago."

"Then I'll see you in the morning." She headed toward the back door. She carried no work with her. Tonight she would not think about murder or Daniel.

Lily would be thrilled by the special treat and Olivia planned to spend the rest of the evening just enjoying her daughter and her mother's company.

She stepped outside the door and into the soupy, humid air. The parking lot was in semidarkness, but the few street lights she could see had come on despite the earliness of the evening.

Her car was parked toward the back of the lot. She usually left the parking spaces closer to the building for the deputies. She hurried toward the car, eager to make the stop at Jimmy's Place and then get home.

She had just reached her car's back bumper when she felt a stir of the otherwise still air. She heard the hurried slap of shoes on the pavement, but before she could turn around, something slammed over her head.

Explosive pain...a shower of stars and then she slumped to the ground in complete darkness.

Chapter Six

"At least Savannah will have a home-cooked meal ready for you," Daniel said to Josh as the two walked out the back door. "I'll have to zap something in the microwave and pretend it's home cooked."

"That's the life of a confirmed bachelor," Josh replied with a laugh.

Daniel thought about sharing dinner with Olivia, her mother and her daughter. It had been far too pleasant and had unsettled him a bit. He'd never thought about how quiet and tasteless most of his evening meals were before.

He wasn't sure now if it had been Rose's cooking or the company that had made the meal so entertaining and wonderful.

He frowned as he saw Olivia's car in the distance. Although she had only preceded them out of the building by a minute or two, she should be pulling out of the lot by now.

"I wonder if Sheriff Bradford is having car problems," he said to Josh. "She should have been on her way by now."

"Maybe we should check it out," Josh replied.

Daniel was grateful that the black clouds overhead had yet to weep a single drop of rain. He and Josh drew closer to Olivia's car and that was when he heard the moan, saw her lying prone on the pavement near her back bumper.

"Olivia!" Daniel's heartbeat went wild in his chest as he hurried to her. By the time he and Josh reached her, she sat up, but appeared dazed.

Daniel crouched down next to her. "What happened? Did you fall?"

"No…no. I was hit over the head." She raised a hand to the top of her head and when she dropped it back to her lap it was bloody. Daniel's heartbeat double-timed in rhythm at the sight of the red stain of blood on her fingers.

"I'll go get some other men to scour the area," Josh exclaimed and quickly turned and ran back toward the building.

Daniel pulled his gun and remained crouched by her side. "We need to get you to the hospital," he said urgently.

"No, that isn't necessary. I'm fine. I was only unconscious for a minute. I don't feel sick and I'm not confused. My head hurts, but I'm okay," she said.

"Are you sure?" Daniel split his attention between her and the dark parking lot, his gun ready if more danger came at them from any direction.

"Really, I'm okay."

By that time half a dozen men had burst out of the

sheriff's station, guns drawn and ready to do whatever necessary to protect their boss.

"Split up and check the area," Daniel instructed as Olivia struggled to her feet.

Daniel took her by the elbow and led her away from her car and to his patrol car. He opened the passenger door and insisted she sit. She did so without argument, and that worried him as much as anything.

"Did you see who it was?" he asked.

"No. I only heard the approach of somebody right before I got whacked. I didn't get a chance to turn around to see who was behind me." She reached up and touched the top of her head again and winced.

In the car light she appeared too pale and still stunned. Daniel wanted to kill whoever was responsible. Flashlight beams filled the lot as the men searched the parking lot and surrounding area.

She stared down at her bloody hand. "I can't go home like this. It will totally freak out my mother and Lily."

"Are you sure you shouldn't go to the hospital?" Daniel asked worriedly.

"No, I don't need a doctor," she replied firmly. "Thank goodness I'm hardheaded."

"You can come to my place and clean up," Daniel suggested and ignored her attempt at humor. He found nothing remotely funny about any of this.

"In fact, I think I should take you there now." He gestured toward the men working in the parking lot. "I'll see that Josh stays here and oversees the sweep of the area." He wanted to get her out of here and some-place safe.

She leaned back against the seat as if relieved to have somebody else momentarily in charge.

Daniel reholstered his gun and walked over to Josh. "Can you take care of things here? I'm going to get her away from here and to my place for the time being."

Josh's features were grim in the faint light. "I can't believe anyone would be so brazen as to attack her here at the station." He looked at the men and nodded. "I'll see to it that every inch of this parking lot and beyond is thoroughly searched for anything that might be evidence."

"I knew I could count on you," Daniel replied.

"Always," Josh replied. "Now get her out of here. If we find anything at all I'll call you and let you know."

"Thanks." Daniel headed back to his patrol car, knowing that Josh would do a thorough job. When he reached his car, Olivia had already closed the passenger door and buckled herself in.

Daniel got in behind the steering wheel and looked at her intently. "I'm going to ask you one last time. Do you need to go to the hospital and have your head checked out?"

"And I'm going to answer that question one final time. I'm shaken up and my head hurts, but I don't need a doctor. Trust me, if I was worried about it I would insist you take me to the hospital."

"Then it's off to my place," he said and started the car. She was silent on the drive and Daniel found himself gazing at her again and again, needing to assure himself that she was really okay.

The vision of her lying on the pavement would stay with him for a long time. His heartbeat still hadn't returned to a normal rhythm. They should have taken the stuffed-dog threat more seriously. Dammit, he should have done something differently so this would have never happened.

Seeing her blood on her hand after she'd touched her head had emphasized the fact that by sheer luck alone she hadn't been hit hard enough to be killed.

Daniel gripped the steering wheel more tightly as a burning rage lit up inside him. Had the perpetrator been Shelly's killer afraid of what the reinvestigation might find? Or, even more chilling, had it been a fellow deputy who was threatened by the internal investigation she was conducting?

All he knew for sure was that he would do everything in his power to see that no more harm came to her. When he reached his house, he pulled into the garage and closed the door behind him.

He got out of the car and hurried around to the passenger side to help her out. She still appeared shaken up, and he took her by the elbow to lead her into the house.

Once inside he guided her down the hallway, through his bedroom and into the master bath. He pointed her to sit on the commode while he grabbed a first aid kit from the nearby linen closet.

He opened it on the edge of the sink and grabbed a bottle of hydrogen peroxide and cotton balls. "I want to take a look at your wound. It's bled quite a bit and it's possible you might need stitches."

"Head injuries always bleed a lot," she replied. She closed her eyes. "Go ahead and do your thing, Dr. Daniel."

He was pleased to hear the touch of lightness in her voice but hated how she winced and released a small moan as he carefully parted her thick dark hair to reveal the area of injury.

He used the peroxide to dab away the excess blood as she sat perfectly still, not making another sound. "The good news is the cut isn't that big," he said when he had removed as much of the blood as possible. "The bad news is you have a nice bird's-egg lump."

"At least it's a bird's egg and not a dinosaur egg," she replied.

He stood too close to her, was able to feel the heat from her body warming his, the scent that managed to muddy his senses if he allowed it to. She'd just been attacked, and he felt as if he was under a sensual assault.

He stumbled back from her at the same time her eyes widened slightly and she stood. "Thank you for cleaning me up," she said as he busied himself returning the first aid kit to the closet.

"All in a day's work for Dr. Daniel. Now, how about a beer?" he asked as they left the bathroom and walked back down the hall toward the kitchen.

"Do you have anything stronger?" she asked. She sank down at a chair at the kitchen table.

He looked at her in surprise. "I have bourbon. Are

you sure that's a good idea? Now that I think about it, maybe a beer isn't a good idea, either."

"A shot of bourbon is a wonderful idea," she replied.

He pulled the bottle of bourbon from the cabinet and then grabbed two glasses and joined her at the table. He poured about an inch of the liquor in each glass and she drank the shot in one swallow. She then gestured for him to pour her another. He hesitated only a moment before pouring her a refill.

This time she wrapped her fingers around the glass and released a deep sigh. Her face was still pale, and more than anything Daniel wanted to draw her into his arms and tell her everything was going to be okay.

But he couldn't tell her that. The attack had come out of nowhere and he had no idea if the intent had been to wound or to kill her.

"Somebody definitely doesn't like me," she finally said.

Daniel offered her a sympathetic smile. "You shouldn't take it personally. I'm pretty sure it's not about you, but rather what you've stirred up here in reopening the murder case."

"Or it was somebody who doesn't like the internal investigation I'm conducting within the department."

"I already thought about that," he admitted. "I know that you've been looking at Ray McClure and Randy Fowler. Ray left the building about a half an hour before you did, and since Randy works the overnight shift, who knows where he was at the time you were attacked." Daniel downed his bourbon. "We'll make sure we know in quick order exactly where they were and what they were doing when you left the building."

He poured himself another shot of the smooth bourbon. "Is there anyone else you're looking at closely within the department?"

She hesitated and took a sip of her drink. "Malcolm Appleton." Daniel raised an eyebrow and she continued. "He recently bought an expensive sports car and has moved into a bigger house. There are definitely some red flags there that I'm looking into."

"Then we check his alibi, too," Daniel replied. He was both surprised and disappointed that in such a small department three of the men were under suspicion. He wasn't surprised that Ray was under scrutiny. He and Trey Walker had been close. But he was surprised by circumstantial evidence that had Randy Fowler and Malcolm Appleton potentially in her sights as dirty cops who might have participated in the drug-trafficking scheme and profited financially.

Olivia had just finished her second drink when Daniel's cell phone rang. Josh's name showed up and he answered. Daniel listened to what his friend had to say and a chill danced up his spine.

"Bag and tag and put it in the evidence room and I'll look at it tomorrow," he said to Josh.

"Bag and tag what?" Olivia asked when Daniel had hung up.

Her eyes were slightly widened and darker than he'd ever seen them. Her body was tensed, as if prepared to take a blow, and he hated that he was about to deliver a definite blow.

"Close to where we found you the men found a piece of evidence," he began.

She leaned forward. "What kind of evidence?"

"A knife. It's possible that the attacker intended to knock you unconscious and then stab you, but when Josh and I came out of the building we interrupted his plans."

A knife. Olivia tried to process Daniel's words in her overworked brain.

She motioned for more bourbon, even though she was already feeling a buzz from the first two drinks. She preferred the buzz to the utter horror that blew an arctic blast of air through her body.

"So it wasn't just an attack, it was an attempted murder," she said. "Thank God you and Josh left the building when you did. If you'd come out just three or four minutes later, you probably would have found me dead."

Daniel reached across the table and took her hand in his. Under no other circumstances would she welcome his touch, but she did so now, curling her fingers with his in an attempt to warm the icy chill that had taken up residency inside her.

"I'm not going to let anything happen to you," he said, his green eyes narrowed with steely determination. "When we got the package with the note and the stuffed animal, none of us knew how serious the threat was. We know now that a threat is real and present and

I'll make sure that nothing like this or anything else happens again to you."

She finally untwined her fingers from his and drew her hand back. She took a drink of the heat of the bourbon and then gazed at him thoughtfully.

"What I don't understand is how killing me would stop anything. Whoever is sent to take my place will continue an investigation into Shelly's death and the internal issues within the department," she said.

Daniel shrugged. "Your murder would certainly take precedence over any other ongoing investigation. Maybe the perp thinks that by hurting or killing you it will buy him some time."

"Time for what? To run? Whoever killed Shelly has had two years to run. Time to cover their tracks? We haven't found any tracks to start to follow," she replied in frustration.

She took another sip of her bourbon and realized she was passing from buzzed to more than slightly inebriated. "Jeez, I can't go home tonight. I'm wounded and I'm just a little bit drunk."

"Then you can stay here tonight," he said without hesitation. "I have an extra room and you can call your mother and tell her you're pulling an all-nighter."

What sounded even better was staying here and sleeping in the warmth and security of Daniel's arms, but she wasn't drunk enough to make that mistake again.

"Are you sure you wouldn't mind?" she asked.

"To be honest, I'd feel better if you stayed. You've

been through a trauma and you don't want to take that home to your mother and daughter."

She nodded, grabbed her purse and reached inside to fumble for her cell phone. Once she had it in hand, she called her mother and told her she'd be working through the night and would be home sometime the next morning.

When she hung up, she stared at the phone for a long moment and then looked at Daniel. "I was going to take Lily mozzarella sticks tonight."

"I can take care of that," Daniel replied, his voice so deep, so soft she wanted to lean her head against his shoulder and just let him take care of everything.

He pulled out his cell phone and within minutes he had called Jimmy's Place for a double order of mozzarella sticks to be delivered to Olivia's house.

"Jimmy has a teenager who works deliveries for him in the evenings," Daniel explained.

Olivia picked up her phone once again. "I'll text Mom to let Lily know a special treat is coming since I won't be home to tuck her in tonight."

She texted the message and then dropped her phone back into her purse. "Let's talk about something other than attacks and murder," she said. Her head ached but she wasn't quite ready to go to bed.

"What do you want to talk about?"

"I don't know…tell me about your family. Are your parents still alive?"

"Yeah, they're alive but I don't have any relationship with them. I haven't had anything to do with them since I turned eighteen." A faint hint of resentment colored his tone.

"Why is that?" she asked curiously.

He swallowed the last of his second glass of bourbon and then leaned back in his chair, tension riding his features. "My parents divorced when I was thirteen, and I became the tool they used to hurt each other for the next five years. It was dirty, it was messy and I swore then that I'd never marry and have children who could be used as pawns if things went bad."

His eyes had gone the moss green of swampy depths. "By the time they finished with me, I didn't like either one of them and I definitely didn't like myself."

"Where are they now?"

"Last I heard my father had moved to California and my mother is in Florida. Neither of them had much use for me when I became legal age and I'd definitely lost all respect for both of them."

"I'm so sorry," Olivia said. She had no idea what it was like growing up with that kind of family dynamics. It was an explanation as to why he was a bachelor and intended to remain so.

"What about you? I know you don't have your father anymore, but did you have a good life growing up?" he asked and some of the shadows lifted from his eyes.

"I had a wonderful family life," she said. "My parents were loving and supportive and I was spoiled to distraction. The worst day of my life was when my father died. He was standing in the kitchen on a Saturday morning making pancakes when he just dropped dead from a massive heart attack. He was gone before anyone could do anything for him."

She ran a finger over the rim of her empty glass. "My mother and I were devastated, and that's when my mother became such a worry wart about me."

"She must hate your job."

Olivia smiled, the gesture renewing the ache in the top of her head. "She does, but she also knows it's not only what I do but who I am. Actually for the most part my mother is almost as innocent as Lily. She believes in the goodness of people and that's part of her charm and why I try to protect her from knowing too much about what I do."

It had been a long monologue and when she finished, she gazed out the window where raindrops had begun to slide down the glass.

Between the trauma that the night had brought and the booze she had consumed, she was suddenly achingly exhausted.

"I think I'd like that spare room now," she said.

Daniel jumped out of his chair and was immediately at her side. He grasped her by an elbow and helped her up and then led her down the hallway into a guest bedroom decorated in shades of blue. He seemed to be holding her by the elbow a lot, guiding her one place or another. But the warmth of his hand on her skin was welcome and made her feel not quite so all alone.

He dropped his hand, and she stood in the doorway as he walked over and lowered a shade at the window and then turned down the bed. "Sit," he said and pointed to the edge of the bed. She obeyed, too exhausted to do anything else. "I'll go get you a T-shirt to sleep in," he said and then disappeared from the bedroom.

She fought the impulse to curl up into a fetal ball. Although she was bone weary and her head throbbed with a dull ache, her brain spun a thousand miles a minute.

She'd been in town just a little over a week and already she'd been threatened by a mutilated stuffed animal and a note and somebody had tried to kill her.

If Josh and Daniel had waited another minute before leaving the station tonight, there was no doubt in her mind that she would have been dead. The perp would have used that knife to stab her to death.

Who had been behind the attack? Had it been somebody they had already interviewed? Somebody still on their list to be interviewed? Or had it been one of the officers she was scrutinizing?

Daniel returned to the room, a folded white T-shirt in his hand. "Thanks," she said as she took it from him.

"The guest bathroom is just across the hall. Everything you need should be there, but if you can't find something let me know."

"I don't know how to thank you for everything you're doing for me."

He smiled softly. "It's all in a day's work. Now, get into bed. You should feel better in the morning, and by then maybe some of the men will have more answers for us."

He left the room and Olivia pulled herself up wearily from the bed and went across the hall to the bathroom.

There was no way she was going to shower tonight, not with her head hurting and the slight wooziness of too much bourbon.

She found a clean washcloth and washed off her face and neck, the warm soapy water doing little to alleviate the cold chill that had been inside her since she came to on the pavement in the parking lot and realized what had happened.

She stripped off her clothes and pulled on the T-shirt that smelled of fresh-air fabric softener and the faint hint of Daniel's cologne.

When she scurried from the bathroom back to the bedroom, she heard Daniel talking softly on the phone in the living room. At the moment she didn't care what he might learn or who he was probably speaking to. She was out of order for the night, and there would be time enough in the morning to deal with whatever needed to be done.

She laid her clothing on a nearby chair, placed her gun on the nightstand within easy reach and then turned off the overhead light. She crawled beneath crisp white sheets and released a deep sigh. Her body relaxed into the unfamiliar mattress, so much more comfortable than the futon at her home where she slept every night.

A soft knock sounded and Daniel opened the door. "All settled in?" he asked and walked to the side of the bed. The light from the hallway spilled into the room, making it easy for her to see his handsome features.

"Just waiting for the Sandman to come and take me

to sleep land," she replied. "Is there any more news? I heard you on the phone a few minutes ago."

"I was just checking in with Josh, and no, there isn't anything new. But you don't have to think about that now." He reached out and pulled the sheet up closer around her neck.

It had been years since Olivia had been tucked into bed by anyone, but what Daniel was doing felt like that. "On a scale of one to ten, ten being the worst day of my life, I'd say this day is hovering around twelve."

Daniel stroked a strand of her hair off her forehead and away from her face and then to her surprise he leaned down and gently kissed her forehead. "Try to get some sleep, Olivia. I swear to you that I'm not going to let anything else happen to you again while you're here in Lost Lagoon."

He turned and left the room, obviously not expecting a reply from her. She couldn't have replied anyway, for a large lump of emotion had jumped into the back of her throat the minute his lips had touched her.

She had a killer after her and a department to clean up, but at the moment equally concerning was the fact that she feared she was falling in love with Lily's "Deputy."

Chapter Seven

It was just after seven the next morning when Daniel heard the water running in the guest bathroom. Olivia was up. He'd been awake, showered and dressed for an hour.

He'd spent that time drinking coffee, making lists of alibis that needed to be checked out for the time of the attack on Olivia and chomping at the bit to get into the office and take a look at the knife that had been found at the scene.

He'd specifically told Josh he didn't want anyone else processing the knife. Daniel knew the odds weren't good that he'd find any fingerprints on it, but items sometimes gave up other evidence.

He'd also made a list of who had been interviewed in the Sinclair murder case and who they had yet to talk to. The other task force members had focused on people who had been on the periphery of Shelly's life, specifically her girlfriends at the time of her death.

He and Olivia had decided early on that the two of them would take on the potential major players in the murder, but they hadn't had enough time yet to talk to anyone except Eric Baptiste.

Things had moved too fast, had spiraled out of control without any real warning. The attack on Olivia now had given a new urgency to everything.

He took a drink of his hot coffee, the liquid adding to the burn that already existed in the pit of his stomach. It was a burn of rage that had begun the moment he'd realized Olivia had been assaulted and might have been killed.

He looked up from his notes as she appeared in the kitchen doorway. Thankfully she looked rested, clear-eyed and determined. "Good morning," he said. "How did you sleep?"

"Like a baby," she replied. She walked over to the counter where a clean cup sat next to the coffeemaker. She helped herself to a cup and then joined him at the table.

"Looks like you've been busy," she said and gestured toward the notes in front of him.

"Just writing down names and thoughts."

"Anything new come up while I slept?" She took a sip of her coffee.

"No, nothing as far as evidence or suspects, but I've come up with a new plan," he replied.

She raised an eyebrow. "A new plan? Sounds interesting."

He gave her a rueful smile. "We'll see how interesting you find it once it's implemented. My plan is that from now on you go no place without me. That means

I follow you to and from the station every day and you aren't out of my sight unless you're safe in your home."

He reached under the papers and pulled out a business card. "This is the rest of the new plan. It's Buck Ranier's card, and I want you to get a security system installed at your house today. Charge it to the department and tell your mother it's standard practice for the sheriffs in Lost Lagoon."

She held the card and stared at it and then slowly nodded her head. "Okay, consider it done."

The fact that she'd acquiesced so easily let him know that she was still frightened, although hiding it very well. "Then I'll go home this morning and get the security system installed. Hopefully it can be done this morning and I can be back at the station by noon," she added.

"And I think the next person we need to interview is Mac Sinclair. He works out of a home office and is some kind of computer tech guru. It's probably a good thing he's his own boss, because rumor is he has a bad temper."

"And we know he didn't like Shelly dating Bo, so he definitely sounds like somebody we need to talk to," she agreed. She took another drink of her coffee. "We need to step up our pace." A faint tension rode her voice, belying the calm of her expression.

"We're going to work as long and as hard as possible to find out who attacked you," Daniel replied in fierce resolve.

"I can't lose track of the reason I'm here. I still need

to find out who is dirty and who isn't in the department and solve Shelly's case," she replied.

"If we find out who attempted to kill you last night, then I believe we'll either know who murdered Shelly or we'll have the identification of a dirty cop. Unless you brought a killer with you from Natchez, then I'm sure the attack on you last night was tied to one of the other two issues."

"So, we continue to work the Sinclair case and I continue the internal investigation and hopefully by solving one of those we'll know who came after me."

"Exactly," Daniel replied.

Olivia finished her coffee and then stood and carried the cup to the sink. "I need to get home and get this security system done so we can get back to the real work."

Daniel got up from the table. "I'll take you back to the station to get your car and then I'll follow you home. When you're ready to return to the station, then call me and I'll tail you from your house back to the station."

She frowned. She obviously wasn't thrilled with his new plan, but he didn't intend to back down. She was his boss, but she was also a woman he cared about and boss or no boss, she was doing this his way.

It was just after nine when Daniel walked into the squad room after following Olivia home. She'd confirmed with Buck to get the security system installed by noon and she was to call Daniel when she was ready to return to work.

Daniel headed directly toward the small evidence

room and found the plastic bag with the knife that had been found by Olivia's body the night before.

He set it in the center of his desk and then sat and stared at it. He instantly identified it. He'd used one dozens of times when eating at Jimmy's Place.

It was a wooden-handled wickedly sharp steak knife with the familiar JP engraved in the handle. Josh pulled up his chair next to Daniel's.

"Not much help," he said. "Anyone who has ever eaten or worked at Jimmy's Place could have taken one of those without anyone being the wiser."

Daniel looked at his friend wryly. "Are you trying to put me in a happy mood as I start a new day?"

"Just sayin'," Josh replied. "I'll be shocked if you get any prints off it."

"Yeah, so will I," Daniel agreed. "But I'll print it anyway and see if the blade holds anything that might tell us something about who was carrying it last night."

"Before you get all involved with that, I need to talk to you about something."

A discordant tone in Josh's voice forced Daniel to give him his undivided attention. Josh's features were troubled. "What, Josh? What's going on?" Daniel hoped to hell Josh wasn't about to confess to having something to do with the drug-trafficking scheme or anything else illegal.

Josh drew in a deep breath and then released it slowly. "I don't know if this has anything to do with anything, but up until last night Savannah had made me promise not to tell anyone."

"Tell anyone about what?" Daniel asked curiously.

Josh stared at the wall just behind Daniel's head. "I don't know, maybe I should have said something before now, but Savannah just wanted to forget the whole thing."

"Forget what?" Daniel asked with a hint of impatience.

Josh focused on Daniel once again. "About a year before Shelly was murdered, Savannah dated Neil Sampson a couple of times. He coerced her into having sex with him before she was ready."

Daniel straightened up. "You mean he raped her?"

"Yes. She didn't want to do anything, but he forced it on her. Savannah thinks it wasn't really rape, though, because she didn't specifically tell him no but 'finally just let it happen' and then never dated him again."

"Oh man, I'm sorry," Daniel said.

"I think she's afraid to come to terms with it." Josh nodded and smiled weakly. "But her telling me is a sign she might be ready to start." His smile faded into a thoughtful frown. "Then last night I got to thinking. Shelly and Savannah looked almost exactly alike, and right before her murder Shelly told her friends that she had a sticky situation on her hands."

"And you're wondering if maybe that sticky situation might have been that Neil Sampson forced himself on her, too?"

"The thought kept me up most of last night," Josh admitted.

"Savannah had already proven that she wasn't going to tell anyone, but Shelly had more friends and was bolder. Neil probably knew that Savannah would be too embarrassed to tell anyone, but Shelly was a wild card."

Daniel rolled the new information over in his brain several times. Was it possible that the handsome, slick city councilman had a secret worth killing for? Was it possible he'd raped Shelly and had been afraid she'd tell somebody?

"I think this just moved Neil up the food chain," he finally said.

"I didn't know anything about the attack on Savannah until we got together, and she wanted me to keep it to myself. I probably should have said something sooner," Josh repeated regretfully.

"You said something now," Daniel replied.

"I'll let you get back to your work on the knife," Josh said and scooted back to his own desk.

It was just after noon when Olivia came through the door. Daniel immediately jumped to his feet and followed her into the office.

He closed the door behind him as she sat behind her desk. "What in the hell do you think you're doing?" he demanded.

"Getting to work," she said briskly.

"You were supposed to call me when you were ready to come in." He was angry with her and the surge of anger inside him surprised him.

"I figured there wouldn't be a problem with me driving from my house to here."

"You figured there wouldn't be a problem walking to your car in the parking lot last night," he countered. He took off his badge and slammed it down on her desk. "I won't stick around and watch you make mistakes that put you in potential danger. You either do this my way or I'm taking the highway." He was somewhat stunned to realize it wasn't an idle threat.

She leaned back in her chair, her brown eyes shining with a hint of amusement. "Are you overly dramatic often?"

Some of the steam left him. "Only when people I care about are involved and are being pigheaded when it comes to their own safety."

She held his gaze for a long moment and in the very depths of her eyes he thought he saw a longing, and desire for her punched him in the gut.

"Put your badge back on, Deputy Carson," she said. "I promise from now on we'll do things your way when it comes to my safety."

"And that's a real promise?"

She leaned forward and raised her right hand. "That's a real promise."

He grabbed his badge and pinned it back on and then sat in the chair across from her desk. "Did you get the security system installed?"

"Buck wired every window and door. I told Mom that the owner of the property wanted it done to protect his investment."

"And she bought it?"

"Hook, line and sinker. Have you had a chance to look at the knife that was found last night?"

Whatever emotion he thought he'd seen in her eyes

was gone and the cool, professional Sheriff Bradford was back in control.

He told her about the knife being from Jimmy's Place and that he'd found no fingerprints or any evidence that it had ever been used for anything. The blade and handle had come up clean and appeared new.

He then told her about the information Josh had shared with him about Neil Sampson. "But it doesn't make sense that he'd kill Shelly because he was afraid of her telling somebody and yet he didn't try to kill Savannah," Olivia said thoughtfully.

"You'd have to know the two sisters. Savannah was always shy and quiet. She didn't have many friends of her own. Neil might have known human nature enough to recognize that Savannah would rather keep it a secret than make any kind of a scene. Shelly, on the other hand, was a much bigger personality. She was a wild card and he might have worried about her...if something happened between them at all."

"There are a lot of ifs in this whole investigation. Maybe we can work in two interviews this afternoon and talk to both Mac and the councilman."

"I'm ready to get started whenever you are," he replied.

"Then let's do it," she said and grabbed her purse.

Oh, he'd love to do it. He'd love to take her home to the bed where she'd slept the night before and have her naked and willing. He'd love to sweep everything off her desk and do it right now.

Instead, they'd spend the afternoon talking to a man

with a bad temper and another man whose ambition might have led to murder.

Mac Sinclair lived in a modest ranch house on the east side of town. His wife, Sheila, opened the door when Olivia knocked. "Sheriff... Daniel...what are you doing here?" Sheila was a small woman with mousy brown hair and shoulders that appeared to be permanently slumped in defeat. Her pale blue eyes held a wealth of anxiety.

"We need to talk to Mac," Daniel said.

Sheila's eyes widened. "He's working right now. Can you come back at another time? He really doesn't like to be disturbed when he's working." She wrung her hands and turned to glance behind her, as if afraid her husband might suddenly appear.

"Working or not, we need to talk to him now," Olivia said firmly.

"He's in the garage. That's his workshop." With obvious reluctance, Sheila opened the door to allow them into a spotlessly clean living room.

They followed her into an equally clean kitchen and she pointed to a door. "He's out there," she said, but didn't open the door to announce them.

Mac must have one hell of a temper, Olivia thought. It was obvious Sheila was fearful of him. There was definitely no accounting for love that would keep a woman with the man she feared. Although in her years of working, Olivia had seen plenty of domestic abuse and women who, far too often, chose to stay with their abusers.

She glanced over at Daniel and thought of their initial conversation when he'd come barreling into the office. She hadn't expected his anger, an anger born in the fact that he cared about her.

But caring wasn't loving and loving wasn't commitment, she reminded herself. She needed to finish her job here and then escape from Daniel before he got any more deeply into her heart.

Thankfully, he hadn't questioned her story about her marriage and immediate pregnancy. Blessedly, he hadn't asked Lily for her precise birth date. She needed to finish up here before she made a mistake that could give away the truth about Lily's parentage.

With that notion in her head, she knocked on the garage door and then opened it. "Mac Sinclair, it's Sheriff Bradford and Deputy Carson," she said.

She and Daniel stepped down to the garage floor. Mac sat at a huge industrial desk surrounded by shelving units that held computer parts and equipment. He frowned as he looked up from a laptop that sat on the desk before him.

He shoved back from the desk, a frown furrowing his brow. "I'd ask what this is about, but I know you're re-investigating Shelly's murder. I don't know why you're wasting your time here to talk to me—we all know who is responsible. We've finally started to heal from this, and here you are to pick the scabs off old wounds."

Mac obviously didn't have a problem speaking his mind. "The investigation at the time of Shelly's murder was done by a dirty cop who rushed to judgment and did a shoddy job," Olivia said. "That's not the way I run things."

Olivia had pegged Mac as a bully, and she wanted him to know without question that she was the new sheriff in town and he wasn't about to bully her. "Now, do you have a couple of chairs where we can sit and talk to you or would you prefer to come down to the station?"

Nobody ever chose to go to the station. She and Daniel stood patiently as Mac got up from his chair, grabbed a couple of folding chairs that leaned against a wall and then opened them.

He was a big man with broad shoulders and hands. It would be easy for him to strangle his sister in a fit of rage and then carry her body to toss it into the nearby lagoon.

"I hear you aren't a big fan of Bo McBride," Olivia said as she and Daniel sat in the chairs and Mac returned to his spot behind the desk.

"Never was. Shelly was too good for him. I told her over and over again that she'd hooked her star to a loser," Mac said. He raked a hand through his thick black hair. "Shelly was smart enough she could have gotten out of this crappy town and made something of herself, but Bo killed her before she got a chance."

"Why would he kill her?" Olivia asked.

Mac shrugged. "Maybe that was the night she finally decided to take my advice and break up with him, and he went nuts."

"Where were you on the night of your sister's murder?" Olivia asked.

Mac stared at her as if she'd lost her mind. "Am I a suspect? Seriously?" His eyes simmered with a barely suppressed anger.

"At this point everyone is a suspect," Daniel said. "So, where were you?"

"I was at home…in bed. I mean at my parents' home."

"The one you and Savannah just sold," Daniel said.

"That's right."

"You were pretty old to still be living at home with your parents," Olivia observed.

"So were Shelly and Savannah," he retorted. "We all were trying to save up money and our parents supported us in the decision to live at home and sock away money. I was trying to get my computer repair business off the ground, Savannah was saving up to open a fine dining restaurant and Shelly was just hoarding her money for whatever she decided to do in the future."

"Did you know that on most nights Shelly and Bo met at the bench by the lagoon to spend a little time together before Shelly worked her night shift at The Pirate's Inn?" Daniel asked.

"Everyone in town knew that. You can't really believe I killed my own sister." Mac's hand on the top of the desk clenched into a fist. "I only wanted what was best for her and that wasn't Bo."

"Maybe it was an accident. Maybe you met her down by the bench to try to get her to break up with Bo and she refused and your anger got the best of you," Daniel said.

"I've heard you have anger control issues," Olivia added, aware that she was baiting the bear.

Mac slammed his fist down on the desk. "You're right, and stupid makes me angry and it's stupid that you are even here talking to me about this. If you believe I killed Shelly, then arrest me, otherwise get the hell out of here and leave me alone. I've got more important things to do with my time."

"He's some piece of work," Olivia said once they were back in her car. "He probably beats his wife every Saturday night just for the fun of it."

"He is a mean bastard," Daniel agreed. "He's always been a bully and possessed a hair-trigger temper, but that doesn't mean he killed Shelly."

"But nothing has taken him off the list of suspects, either." Olivia fought against a wave of frustration. "I guess it's time to talk to the illustrious Neil Sampson and see what he has to offer."

Nothing. Neil was arrogant and openly talked about his brief dating of Savannah, but indicated she had wanted to have sex with him as much as he had with her. He denied having anything to do with Shelly and didn't remember what he had been doing or who he might have been with on the night that Shelly was killed.

It was just after four when they returned to the station. Daniel went to check in with the task force team while Olivia closed herself off in her office to write up reports.

She was determined that even if they didn't solve Shelly's murder before her time in Lost Lagoon ended, the next sheriff would find the files as complete and detailed as possible.

Besides, working on reports kept her mind off Daniel. He'd been so kind to her the night before. He'd tucked her into bed and the gentle kiss he'd delivered to her forehead had made her want to pull him into the bed with her.

Shock and trauma, that was all it had been. She'd been frightened and it was only natural that she'd want somebody to hold her.

The problem was she didn't just want anyone to hold her, she'd wanted Daniel, specifically. If she were smart she'd completely distance herself from him, but he'd now appointed himself her personal bodyguard and the truth was he was the only person in the department she trusted implicitly.

After five, he knocked on her door and came into the office. "Time for all good sheriffs to go home for the day and spend their evening with their family," he said. "By the way, you never told me if Lily enjoyed her mozzarella sticks last night."

Olivia laughed. "She definitely enjoyed them. She asked me when I got home this morning when I'd have to work at night again and she could have more mozzarella sticks." She grabbed her purse and stood. "And, yes, you're right. It's time for me to go home and for you to knock off work for the night."

They walked out of the building together. Daniel

dropped his hand to the butt of his gun, letting her know he was taking his bodyguard duty very seriously.

She was definitely comforted knowing somebody had her back. Even though she hadn't come into the station until noon and it was only a little after five now, she was eager to get home and kiss her mom, hug her daughter and forget about men with bad tempers and a case with no leading suspects.

She didn't want to think about steak knives or an attack in the parking lot. Tomorrow she would be Sheriff Bradford again, but tonight she just wanted to be Olivia, Rose's loving daughter and mother to beautiful little Lily.

She was vaguely surprised when she pulled into the driveway at her house and Daniel parked just behind her and got out of his car. She exited her car and stood by the driver door until he joined her.

"Did you forget something?" she asked.

"No, I just figured I'd see a lady to her door," he replied.

"I'm not a lady, I'm your boss," she retorted with a smile.

"I have a terrible confession to make," he said as they reached her small front porch.

She pulled her house key from her purse and looked at him cautiously. "A confession?"

He nodded. "I have to confess that from the moment my new boss showed up, I've wanted to kiss her."

"You kissed me last night on the forehead." Warmth filled her cheeks as she thought of that tender kiss.

"That's not the kind of kiss I'm thinking about," he replied and took a step closer to her.

She was playing with fire and she knew it but was unable to help herself. "Then what kind of kiss have you been thinking about?" she asked, her heartbeat speeding up.

"This kind." He pulled her into his arms and slanted his lips down to hers.

Memories cascaded through her head as she parted her lips to allow him to deepen the kiss. Laughter as they'd nearly tripped over each other in their eagerness to undress. White hot desire had stolen the laughter as they'd fallen onto the hotel bed.

Those memories fell away as the here and now intruded and the fiery heat she tasted in his lips snapped her back to the present. His tongue twirled with hers, creating a flame of want in the pit of her stomach.

She wanted to fall against him, meld her body with his until she didn't know where she began and he ended. Her overwhelming desire for him and the fact that they were out in the open on her porch was what forced her to break the kiss and step back from him.

She turned quickly and put her key in the door lock. "Good night, Daniel," she said without turning around.

"Good night, Olivia."

She escaped into the house and immediately punched the code into the keypad to unarm the alarm. Then, with fingers shaking, she reset the alarm.

"Mommy, you're home," Lily came rushing toward her, and Olivia picked her daughter up in her arms and squeezed her tight, a wealth of emotion rising up the back of her throat.

"Is everything all right, dear?" Rose asked as she eyed her daughter.

"Fine, everything is just fine," Olivia assured her with a forced smile. "I'm just glad to be home and I'm ready to spend the evening with the two most important people in my life."

But everything wasn't fine. She had a killer after her and she was head over heels for the man who was Lily's father, a man who didn't even know he had a daughter.

She recognized now that she would walk away from Lost Lagoon with a broken heart…if the killer didn't succeed and she was able to walk away at all.

Chapter Eight

For the last week things had gotten weird. Daniel sat at his desk and stared toward the closed office door. He and Olivia had continued to work together each day and he'd followed her to and from the station, but she'd definitely been distant and a different kind of tension had sprung up between them.

It had been the kiss. It had been hot and sweet and had left him wanting so much more. It had also obviously been a big mistake, creating an awkwardness between them that he now both hated and regretted.

The problem wasn't that she hadn't responded to the kiss. She had. She'd responded with a fiery desire to match his. They just hadn't talked about it the next day or any day since.

They'd spent the week talking to people, checking out alibis and interviewing Jimmy Tambor about the knife that had been found. Jimmy had nothing to offer them. The knives were not only served with a variety of meals, but also kept in a silverware container where the diners could just grab one if needed.

Dead ends. Daniel stared down at the list of names

on his desk. It was a short list of potential suspects. At the top was Eric Baptiste, who had become friends with Shelly just before her death. Second on the list was Mac Sinclair. Shelly wouldn't have been afraid to meet her brother at the bench by the swamp in the middle of the night.

Last on the list was Neil Sampson, a long shot but given his brief relationship with Savannah Sinclair and the fact that Shelly had mentioned she had a sticky situation on her hands, he had made the list. Bo wasn't listed as a suspect, but he wasn't completely cleared, either. It was just a gut instinct that both Daniel and Olivia shared that he was innocent.

Frustration welled up inside Daniel. It was possible the person who had murdered Shelly wasn't even on the damned list. To further the insult of the stymied investigation into Shelly's death was the fact that they had not gotten any closer to finding the person who had delivered the trashed dog or had attacked Olivia.

He looked up to see Deputy Emma Carpenter knocking on Olivia's door. She entered and closed the door behind her. For the past six mornings, Olivia had been calling in the deputies one by one for interviews.

Daniel had no idea what kind of timeline Olivia had here in Lost Lagoon. He did know that when she finished her internal investigation into any corruption left in the department, then a special election would be held for a new sheriff and she would return to her home in Natchez.

It was as if for the past week she'd been working

especially hard on the internal investigation and not as much on the Sinclair case. It was as if she was suddenly eager to put Lost Lagoon…and him behind her.

He shouldn't have kissed her. But she'd looked so darned kissable, and he'd been unable to stop himself from following through on his need to taste her sweet lips again.

He stared back down at his desk, surprised to realize how much he would miss her. He'd grown accustomed to her face being the first one he saw each morning and most evenings the last one he saw before heading home.

Josh rolled his chair over to Daniel's desk. "You know, I've been thinking," he began.

"There's a novel thing," Daniel replied.

"Very funny. Actually, I've been thinking about our suspects in the Sinclair case and the missing engagement ring."

"What about it?" Daniel looked at his friend and fellow worker curiously.

"I'm just trying to figure out who would have a motive to take the ring off her finger. I don't see Neil Sampson having any motive. Mac definitely jumps to the top of the list. He hated Bo and he hated his sister's relationship with him. As far as Eric, maybe it's possible he was in love with Shelly and tried to get her to break up with Bo and when she refused, he killed her and took the ring."

"Sheriff Bradford and I have had the same kind of thoughts," Daniel agreed. "Taking the ring was definitely personal. I suppose it's also possible that Shelly broke up with Bo that night and gave him back the ring."

"I know that Bo had that kind of bad-boy aura going on for him, but he'd never gotten into any trouble. He'd never shown any kind of anger issues. I don't believe he was capable under any circumstances of killing Shelly," Josh replied.

"But we still have to consider him a possibility. We're basically just chasing our tails and running around in circles," Daniel replied with irritation. "Maybe what we need to do is put out the word that we're getting close to making an arrest."

"And hope the perp gets nervous enough to make a mistake? It might work," Josh agreed thoughtfully.

"I'll need to run the idea by Sheriff Bradford," Daniel said.

It was just before five when Daniel knocked on Olivia's door. At her beckoning, he entered and closed the door behind him. "It's almost time to head home, but I wanted to talk to you about a couple of things before we leave."

"What's up?" she asked briskly.

He first told her about his idea to hopefully ferret out the killer. "We can just mention to a couple of people that some new evidence has come to light and we're about to make an arrest. The active rumor mill in town will do the rest for us. Within hours of us putting out the word, everyone in town will hear the news."

"It might work," she said slowly...thoughtfully. "Why don't we have lunch at Jimmy's Place tomorrow? That seems to be the heart of the rumor mill here in town."

"Sounds like a plan," he agreed. "And now let's talk about the kiss."

Her dark eyes widened and she busied herself straightening file folders on her desk. "There's nothing to talk about."

"I disagree. It's created awkwardness between us. You've been distant and different with me since then."

She stopped her busy work, clasped her hands together on top of her desk and gazed at him. "You're right. It has been awkward and I have been trying to distance myself from you."

"Then I'm sorry I kissed you," he replied.

"Don't be… I mean, it wasn't just you, I did kiss you back." Her cheeks flushed pink. "It just brought up memories of being with you in New Orleans and we know we can't go there again."

He wanted to go there again, but he also didn't want to pressure her in any way. "Olivia, I promise I won't kiss you again unless you want me to. I don't want this barrier between us anymore. I want you to be able to trust me on all levels."

She offered him a small smile. "Okay then, we're good."

It took only fifteen minutes for Daniel to follow her home and then walk her to her front porch. The door flew open. "Deputy!" Lily said in obvious excitement. She stepped out of the door and grabbed Daniel's hand and pulled him into the house.

Olivia quickly went to the keypad to deal with the

alarm as Daniel looked down at the little girl whose hand was so warm, so trusting in his.

"I been wondering when you'd come to visit again," Lily exclaimed. "You can eat dinner with us, right, Nanny?"

Rose smiled a hello to him. "There's always plenty for another plate on the table."

"Oh, no, I couldn't," Daniel protested, despite the fact that the scent of tomatoes and garlic had his stomach rumbling.

"But you can, Nanny said it was okay and Mommy wants you to stay, too," Lily exclaimed. "Right, Mommy?"

Daniel looked at Olivia helplessly. She shrugged, took off her gun belt and placed it on top of the cabinet and then sat down on the futon. "You're here now, you might as well stay for dinner." She looked at her daughter. "And where is my greeting? Am I just chopped liver when Deputy Carson is around?"

"Ewww, liver. Yuck." Lily dropped Daniel's hand and rushed to her mother, laughing as she barreled into Olivia and toppled her over to her side. "You aren't chopped liver. I hate liver, but I love, love you!" Lily exclaimed.

Daniel's heart squeezed as mother and daughter laughed together and the heat of Lily's hand remained like a lingering tiny ghost touch in his hand.

He cleared his throat and turned to Rose. "What can I do to help?" he asked. Since he was an unplanned guest, he could at least make himself useful.

Rose pointed to a nearby cabinet. "You can get down

another plate and add it to the table. I hope you like spaghetti, because that's what's on the menu for the night."

"Homemade sauce?" he ventured.

She grinned at him. "Is there any other kind?"

"Excellent." Daniel got down the extra plate and added silverware as Olivia and Lily disappeared into Rose's bedroom, presumably for Olivia to change from her work clothes into something more comfortable.

As Daniel filled glasses with ice and water, he and Rose talked about their mutual love of Italian food, the knitted hats she made and donated for cancer victims and how much she loved her daughter and granddaughter.

By the time Olivia and Lily had returned to the living room, Olivia clad in a pair of pink capris and a white T-shirt with a pink design on the front.

Lily danced right to Daniel's side and once again slipped her hand into his. "You have to come and see the new baby doll Nanny bought for me." She pulled Daniel down so that she could whisper in his ear. "She pees her pants when I give her a bottle of water."

"Five minutes and this will all be on the table," Rose called as Lily led Daniel into her bedroom.

For the next five minutes, Lily enchanted Daniel. He saw the peeing doll and a new dress Olivia had ordered for her, and she talked about everything she had done since the last time he'd seen her.

It was impossible to think about murders and dirty cops when in Lily's world, where fairies danced and pixies played and all things were possible. It was a world of innocence and light that Daniel was almost reluctant to leave when Rose called them to the table.

The light mood continued through dinner. There was a crisp green salad, thick slices of garlic bread and a huge pot of spaghetti.

The spaghetti sauce was the best Daniel had ever tasted. He tried to get the recipe from Rose, who remained smiling but tight-lipped as she insisted it was an old family secret.

There was plenty of laughter as Lily showed Daniel how to slurp spaghetti noodles, her mouth quickly becoming covered in the red sauce. Olivia showed her playful side by challenging her daughter to a slurping contest.

Rose looked on with mock sternness and mumbled about bad manners while Daniel laughed at the antics of mother and daughter.

This was the way family was supposed to be. Meals shared in laughter, happy greetings at the front door after time away from one another. A warmth of caring in the room with everyone together.

Daniel could scarcely remember a meal with his mother and father where one or the other of them hadn't stormed away from the table in anger. The happiness and love in this house was normal. What he had experienced in his childhood had definitely been abnormal. But it had shaped him into the man he'd become.

After dinner Daniel insisted he help with the cleanup, and then it was time for him to leave. He was surprised to realize he didn't want to go back to his silent home where there was no laughter, no whisper of another person's voice.

He'd always been fine alone, but tonight the thought of going back to his quiet house wasn't as appealing as it had always been.

Olivia unarmed the security system and walked out on the front porch with him. "Thanks for dinner," he said.

"Not a problem. As far as Mom is concerned, the more the merrier when it comes to meals. Besides, it was fun and now I have to go inside and tell Lily that it really isn't proper to slurp spaghetti," she said ruefully.

He laughed. "Good luck with that."

She smiled and then sobered, her eyes unusually dark as she gazed up at him. "So tomorrow we try our new strategy," she said.

Just that quickly the pleasant evening faded, replaced by the grimness of murder and the attack on her. He nodded. "Tomorrow we bait a killer and see if he comes out to play."

IT WAS JUST after noon when Olivia and Daniel entered Jimmy's Place the next day. Olivia had spent a restless night tossing and turning as she'd played and replayed the time Daniel had spent with Lily.

He would make a wonderful father, and once again she'd found herself wrestling with the idea of telling him the truth about Lily. Still, she'd awakened this morning once again strong in her resolve to keep his fatherhood a secret.

One night of him eating dinner with them, laughing with Lily and enjoying her company did not a father make, she told herself firmly. This was one secret she had to keep to herself.

She had interviewed nearly all the men in the department and had yet to find direct evidence that any of them had been involved in corruption of any kind.

Malcolm Appleton had explained his new financial situation by showing her a copy of a check that had come from his late father's estate. Richard Appleton had been a wealthy man who had passed away from cancer and left everything to his only son, Malcolm.

The only one who seemed to have come into a recent inexplicable windfall was Randy Fowler, who had not only managed to move his ailing mother into a nice nursing home facility, but had also bought a new house for himself and his wife and two children. When questioned about his uptick in finances, he'd been vague and hadn't really given her a real answer.

His bank records showed three six-figure deposits in the last six months from an account under the name of Jesse Leachman and Associates, but so far Olivia hadn't been able to find out anything about just who or what Jesse Leachman and Associates were and why they would be paying Randy anything.

Jimmy Tambor's cheerful smile pulled her from her thoughts of the morning and to the present. "A booth?" he asked.

"Or a table, either is fine," Daniel replied.

They were seated at a table just to the left of the center of the bar and grill, a place where they would easily be seen and overheard if they spoke loud enough.

Nerves bounced in her stomach as they placed their drink orders. What they were going to do wasn't without its dangers. A killer who believed himself safe was much less lethal than one who believed he might possibly be cornered.

If it was Shelly's killer who had attacked her in the parking lot, then he had acted precipitously, driven by the reopening of the case. Now he would be acting out of fear, and that always made people more dangerous.

"Don't look so nervous," Daniel said softly.

"Does it show?"

He smiled. "Probably only to me, but we're going nowhere in the investigation and I think this is our best next move."

"It's his next move that worries me," she replied.

"I've got your back, Olivia."

"I know, but I also don't want you to get in any cross fire." She took a sip of iced water. "If I had my way, it would be just the killer and me and I wouldn't hesitate to pull my trigger."

Daniel's jaw tightened. "This crime has haunted this town for too long. With the amusement park about to breathe new life here, we need to clean up this murder case."

Olivia leaned back in her chair and eyed him wryly. "If anyone was to look at us now and read our expressions, they would assume we're both frustrated and angry at our lack of progress."

"You're right," he agreed. "Maybe we should have ordered a bottle of champagne to make it look like a real celebration."

Olivia laughed. "You know I'm a lightweight when it comes to alcohol. I think we're better off toasting with sweet tea."

The waitress appeared to take their food orders and when she left, Daniel slumped into a position of complete relaxation, a pleasant smile on his face. "So, did you manage to give Lily spaghetti etiquette last night after I left?"

"I didn't have to. Once I got back into the house she told me that she knew that wasn't really the way to eat spaghetti when we were out in public. Apparently, my mother had already had a little discussion with her."

He smiled. "And did your mother have a little discussion with you, because as I remember it you were in on the hijinks, as well."

"Guilty as charged. I told Lily that Nanny didn't need to have a talk with me. I knew both of us had shown bad manners."

"She's a bright kid."

"Oh I don't know, she seems to have taken quite a shine to you," Olivia said teasingly.

"I love a woman with good taste," he replied.

The conversation halted as the waitress arrived with their food orders. While they ate they focused on laughing a lot, appearing confident and at ease. She hoped that it appeared to everyone in the place as if they had the world, or in this instance the case, by the tail.

They were halfway through the meal when Jimmy stopped by their table. "Hi, Sheriff Bradford… Daniel. I just thought I'd stop by to see how you're enjoying your meals. Everything all right here?"

"As usual, the food is excellent and everything is better than okay," Daniel replied. He leaned toward Jimmy. "We caught a big break on Shelly's murder case. It's just a matter of time before we make an arrest."

Jimmy's boyish features radiated surprise and he leaned closer to Daniel. "Is it Eric Baptiste?"

"We can't say anything right now," Olivia said coyly.

"It's Eric, I know it is. He's always been kind of strange and so intense. The only friend he ever had was Shelly and he knew about the tunnels that ran from the Sinclair house to the lagoon." Jimmy straightened. "Don't worry, I won't say anything to anyone."

"And so begins the rumor mill," Daniel said as Jimmy moved away from their table.

"And hopefully the beginning of the end where Shelly's case is concerned," she replied.

"How is the internal investigation going?"

"I'm waiting for confirmation on a couple of things and then I should be able to wrap things up pretty quickly."

"I already miss you."

She averted her gaze from his. "Daniel, you shouldn't say things like that."

"I know I shouldn't, but it's the truth. I've enjoyed

getting to know you better and getting to know your family. I've enjoyed working with you."

She looked back at him and tried not to fall into the lush green depths of his eyes, the evocative warmth of his smile. "I'm not gone yet," she replied.

She focused on the half of a club sandwich left on the plate in front of her. It was nice that he liked spending time with her. It was ridiculous how hot she knew he was to sleep with her again. It was wonderful that he thought Lily was beautiful and charming and that her mother was warm and caring.

None of that changed the truth, and the truth was he could never be a part of her life. He had no desire to be a real part of her life. He was a temporary man and she was working a temporary position in a town that wasn't her home. She was doomed to his being nothing more than a passing ship in the night just as she thought he'd been years ago.

It had been a cruel twist of fate to bring him back into her life now with Lily hungry for a daddy and her ready to move on from the heartbreak of losing one of the most caring men she'd ever known.

They were back at the station just after one, Olivia in her office and Daniel holed up in the small conference room with the rest of the task force.

Would their ruse work? Would the killer now do something that would bring him out into the open? There was no question that she was concerned about what might happen next. She couldn't foresee what consequences she and Daniel had put into motion, but she knew one of the outcomes would be a target directly on her back.

She'd already been attacked once. She just hoped that she and Daniel saw the next one coming if and when it did. From the moment Lily had been born and Olivia had returned to her work in law enforcement, she'd done everything she could to be careful, to be wary. Lily was her reason to stay alive. Olivia wanted to do her job well, but she also wanted to go home each night to her daughter and mother.

At around three o'clock, Mayor Frank Kean entered her office. Olivia greeted him and he sat in the chair opposite her desk, his features wreathed in a smile. "I hear you're close to an arrest in the Sinclair case."

Daniel had been right—the grapevine was alive and well in Lost Lagoon. "We're definitely close," she replied. She hated to lie to the mayor, but she didn't know him well enough to be sure she could trust him with the truth of what they were doing.

"Want to give me the details?"

In Olivia's special capacity here in Lost Lagoon, she didn't have to answer to the mayor as she normally would as an elected sheriff.

"At this point I'd rather not get specific. However, I promise you that if it's possible you'll know before anyone else when we make the arrest."

"I'd appreciate it," he replied. "When the special elections come up, I'm thinking about running for mayor again. I served this town in that capacity for eight years before Jim Burns beat me, and everyone knows how that turned out. My heart is in this town."

Olivia smiled at the older man. "I'm sure you'd be a fine mayor again."

"Have you heard of anyone who plans to run for sheriff after you leave?"

"No, although it's possible Deputy Carson might be interested since he served as interim sheriff before I arrived," she replied.

Frank nodded in approval. "Daniel is a good man. He would make a good sheriff, and I know he has the best interest of Lost Lagoon at heart. Has he mentioned wanting to run?"

"No, we haven't discussed it," she replied. "We've been so busy with the investigation into Shelly's murder."

He leaned forward and gave her a charming smile. "Sure you don't want to give me a hint about who the murderer is?"

Olivia laughed and shook her head. "No matter how much you attempt to charm me, my lips are sealed until we have the culprit under arrest."

"Then I guess I should let you get back to work," he said and stood.

"I promise, I'll keep you informed," she said as he opened the office door to leave. She breathed a sigh of relief the second he stepped out and closed the door behind him.

She had no idea what this newest plan of theirs might

stir up. She couldn't begin to guess whether it would be successful or not.

She was aware that if it was successful, then something bad was probably going to happen very soon.

Chapter Nine

It had been another long day. Daniel and Olivia had spent most of the morning out on the streets, drifting in and out of shops, listening to the gossip on the street and waiting…waiting for something to happen.

They'd eaten lunch at Jimmy's Place and then had returned to the station where Olivia had holed up in her office and Daniel had sat at his desk studying again and again the files and information they'd gathered about Shelly's murder to see if anything or anyone had been overlooked.

He'd gathered everyone's alibis for the night that Olivia had been attacked in the parking lot from the other members of the task force and needed to share the information with Olivia. She wouldn't be pleased by the fact that several of the men had unsubstantiated alibis.

After five, he knocked on her office door. He entered the office to find her staring out the window. She turned when he called her name.

"Sorry," she said, a faint flush of color filling her cheeks. "I was lost in my own head for a few minutes." She looked at her wristwatch. "And it's time to go home."

"I have another offer for you," he said. "I've got cold beer in my refrigerator and a frozen pizza. Why don't we go to my place and do a little brainstorming?"

She hesitated.

"I've finally gotten all the alibis from the suspects we had concerning your attack in the parking lot," he continued as an added incentive.

"Okay," she relented. "Pizza and beer and brainstorming and then I go home."

"Of course," he agreed. "I'll follow you to my place."

It wasn't long before he drove behind her car toward his house. He hadn't realized how much he'd wanted her to come over until the moment he'd asked her. He hadn't realized how lonely his evenings now seemed since he'd shared dinner with her and Lily and Rose a couple of times.

Maybe before this was all finished and before she left town, he'd throw a big pizza party with Rose and Lily included. He'd go all out and order the pizza from Jimmy's Place. An inward smile lit his heart as he thought of Lily stringing cheese down her chin, her green eyes twinkling with happiness while she enjoyed a piece of Jimmy's pizza or a big order of mozzarella sticks just for her.

Olivia was lucky to come home to a loving child and mother each evening. This thought surprised him. He'd never yearned for a family before. He'd always been comfortable in his aloneness. He didn't have to answer to anyone else and had always relished the quiet and peace of being alone after a day at work.

Something had changed. The silence in the evenings now felt a bit stifling. Maybe this new attitude had begun when Josh had hooked up with Savannah Sinclair.

He'd seen his friend and partner happier than ever in love with Savannah. Josh rushed home in the evenings to share dinner with her, to spend time with her. It was obvious he believed he'd met his soul mate and he and Savannah were making plans not only for a wedding, but also for a family.

Daniel had never thought about finding a soul mate, a woman who could fill his life with love and laughter, with shared secrets and passion.

Something about Olivia and her little family definitely had him rethinking his confirmed bachelorhood. Or was it that he was just feeling the loss of Josh in his life? The two had often spent dinner together at Jimmy's or hung out for drinks after work, shortening the time of silence Daniel would have to face when he came home each evening.

He shoved all these thoughts out of his head as he opened both garage doors and Olivia pulled into the garage on the right and he drove into his place on the left.

When they were both out of their cars, he closed the doors and together they went into the kitchen. He turned on the overhead light and motioned her to the table. "Sit and relax and I'll set the oven to preheat."

She removed her gun belt and placed it on the floor

and then sat at the table in the same chair she had when she'd last been there. She placed her purse on the floor next to her gun and holster and then smiled at him. "I hope this isn't one of those cheap, cardboard pizzas. I'm not that kind of girl."

"Of course not," he replied with mock indignation. "It has a rising crust and a trio of meat toppings." He grabbed a couple of beer bottles from the refrigerator and carried them over to the table.

She unscrewed the top and took a drink, then set the bottle back on the table and released a deep sigh. "I expected something to happen by now."

He took the top off his bottle and tossed it into the nearby trash can. "I have to admit, I did, too." He set his beer bottle on the table and grabbed a pizza stone from under the cabinet and then walked back to the refrigerator and took a boxed pizza out of the freezer.

It took him only a minute to pull the pizza from its wrapping and set it on the pizza stone. He turned to look at her. "To be honest, I don't know if I'm disappointed or relieved that nothing has happened so far."

"I'm on pins and needles," she confessed. "The waiting to see what happens is driving me half-crazy. I'm jumping at shadows. You said you had alibis for the time I was attacked in the parking lot?"

He sat across from her at the table, took a sip of his beer and nodded. "Eric Baptiste was at the swamp gathering herbs and roots for his mother. Unfortunately, nobody saw him there. Mac's wife swore that he was home with her at the time in question. Bo and Claire were having dinner at Jimmy's Place and were seen there by several people. The last person I had checked out was Ray McClure."

Olivia raised an eyebrow and at the same time the oven dinged to announce that it had reached the appropriate temperature. Daniel got up from the table.

"I had Ray checked out just because something about him has always rubbed me the wrong way. He's the one person in the department I've never really trusted."

"Besides, he's the one who found the package with the dog inside," Olivia said.

"A package he could have easily put together and brought to your office," Daniel replied. "We only have his word that he just happened to see it in front of the building."

"So, what was his alibi?" she asked.

Daniel shoved the pizza stone into the oven and then returned to the table. "He left the station approximately thirty minutes before you did. He says he went directly home, drank a few beers and didn't have any interaction with anyone that night."

"So the only person who has a definite, solid alibi is Bo."

"That's about the size of it," Daniel agreed.

"If Bo wasn't the one who attacked me, then I definitely don't believe he killed Shelly," she said thoughtfully and took another sip of her beer.

"I always doubted that Bo was responsible," Daniel agreed.

She frowned and reached up to the clip that held her

long dark hair in a tight ponytail at the nape of her neck. "If you don't mind…" She took the clasp off with a sigh of relief. "By this time of the day having my hair held so tight always gives me a bit of a headache."

Did he mind? He reveled in the sight of her lush dark hair falling around her shoulders and his fingers itched with the desire to touch those strands, to feel them wrapped around his hands.

He jumped up from the table and went to the oven to check on the pizza. The heat of the oven had nothing to do with the heat that burned in his belly, a heat of want to take her to bed.

Pizza, beer and a little shoptalk—that's all she signed up for, he reminded himself. "Just another couple of minutes or so and this should be done," he said. He leaned against the cabinet next to the oven.

"How's the investigation into the deputies going?" he asked, desperate to get his mind on anything other than the very hot images of the two of them together in his bed that was shooting off like fireworks in his head.

"Thankfully, I've pretty well cleared everyone of any wrongdoing. My last challenge was Randy Fowler, who finally came clean to me this afternoon when I spoke with him. He'd received several large direct deposit payments into his bank account over the past couple of months from a company called Jesse Leachman and Associates. When I first questioned him about them, Randy was vague and mysterious."

"Hold that thought." Daniel pulled the pizza from the oven, set it on a hot pad on the nearby countertop and then used a pizza slicer to cut it into eight pieces. He then carried it to the table, got plates and napkins and finally sat back down.

"Okay, now tell me the mystery about Randy's money," he said.

"It's a structured settlement from a drug company. He was embarrassed to talk about it because apparently he had been on a drug that was pulled off the market because the side effects messed up...uh...male performance."

Daniel stared at her. "For real?"

"For real. He'll receive checks for the next year and by then he hopes the side effects will wear off. I checked it out. I finally managed to speak to several lawyers at Jesse Leachman and Associates, who faxed me over court documents confirming what Randy had told me."

Daniel gestured for her to take a piece of the pizza. "Well, it's a relief to know it isn't dirty money."

"You can't tell anyone about it." Olivia pulled a piece of the pie onto her plate. "He was mortified to have to tell me about it."

"I can imagine. Men don't like to talk about their sex lives unless they're bragging or lying," Daniel said jokingly.

For the next couple of minutes they ate and stayed silent. Daniel tried everything in his power not to think about his sex life with the woman sitting across from him.

"Maybe one evening we could take Lily and your

mother to the ice cream parlor," he said in an attempt to get inappropriate thoughts out of his head.

She smiled, that warm, open smile of a sexy woman that had nothing to do with Sheriff Bradford. "I'd like that. I was planning on taking them before the attack in the parking lot, but that changed everything and of course I haven't been allowed to leave the house without my deputy escort."

"Maybe your deputy escort could arrange for an ice cream date tomorrow night after work," he replied.

"That would be nice," she replied and then frowned. "As long as you think it's okay for all of us to be out and about."

"I don't think our man will try anything in a public setting. Besides, trust me, nobody is going to hurt you or anyone you love as long as I'm with you."

Unable to stop himself, he reached across the table and grabbed one of her hands with his. He half expected her to pull away, but instead she curled her fingers with his. Their gazes remained locked for several heart-stopping seconds, and then she finally pulled her hand away from his.

"You know I really don't need your bodyguard detail." Her eyes had grown dark and she straightened her back against the chair. "I'm not a poor damsel in distress. I'm a trained officer of the law and I know how to take care of myself. I've faced a lot of bad actors in my career and I'm still here. I'm good at my job."

Sheriff Bradford was definitely present and in the room, Daniel thought. "Olivia, I'm quite aware that you aren't a damsel in distress. I'm not shadowing you because I think you're not capable. We've been working as partners and knowing that somebody has a target on you, I'm acting as any partner would. I've got your back and I would do the same thing for any of the men I was partnered with."

She studied his features for a long moment and then relaxed her shoulders and the darkness in her eyes lightened. "All right then, just so that we're clear."

"We're clear, now eat another piece of pizza and I'll grab us each another beer." He got up from the table and grabbed two more beers from the fridge.

Every word he'd told her was the absolute truth. He'd do the same thing for any man in the department who found himself at the heart of a dangerous investigation.

What he hadn't mentioned was that part of the reason he had insinuated himself into her life as much as he had was because he liked her and he liked her family.

There had been women in his past, but none had ever stirred such a fierce need to protect like she did inside him. He didn't remember ever feeling this way about any other woman, and it confused him.

He told himself it was because he couldn't forget the passion-filled night he'd experienced with her five years ago.

He couldn't ignore how much he wanted that same experience again. It was easier to chalk it up to lust, and that thought made it okay for him to want her once again.

OLIVIA GRABBED A second piece of pizza and tried to ignore the overwhelming pull she experienced whenever she was around Daniel.

Five years ago he'd been a sexy man in a bar offering her a night of sex, a night of temporary forgetfulness of her grief over her partner's death. He'd been a one-dimensional man who had unexpectedly wound up being the father of her daughter due to their carelessness.

He was so much more now. She admired his intelligence. He was a man of honor and committed to his job and the town he served. He respected her as his boss, but also saw and respected the woman behind the badge.

She wanted him again. Not as a husband, not as a committed boyfriend—she knew better than to wish for such things from him. But, she definitely wanted him again.

And she knew without a doubt that he desired her, too. He'd done little to hide it. It was in his eyes when he gazed at her, in the heat of his hands when he touched her in even the most simple way. It had definitely been in the kiss they had shared. It would be just a one-night stand, just like it had been years ago. Only this time she was aware that her heart would be involved.

Still, she had no illusions. If they did make love again, it would only be a memory she'd take back to Natchez with her. It wouldn't be the beginning of anything between them.

"You've gotten very quiet," Daniel said, pulling her from her thoughts.

She stared at him for a long moment. If she said what

she wanted to say, then there would be no going back. She needed to be sure of what she wanted to happen. She was sure.

"I was just thinking about us making love again," she said.

The piece of pizza he'd been about to bite into hung midair between his plate and his mouth. His eyes widened and then narrowed. "And what, exactly, were you thinking about it?"

"That it would be wrong on all kinds of levels, but I still want it to happen."

He slowly lowered his slice of pizza to his plate, his gaze locked with hers. "Do you have a specific time in mind for this to happen?"

Her heart suddenly thundered with the anticipation of what she was about to set into motion. "I was thinking maybe after we finish eating."

He shoved his plate away. "I'm full."

Olivia fought the impulse to laugh, but his actions and words fired a heat of want through her, a want she had battled since the moment she'd walked into the sheriff's office and seen him again.

"I'm finished eating, too," she replied, surprised that her voice was half-breathless.

"Then why are we still sitting here at the table?" He got out of his chair and walked around to her. He pulled her up and into his arms.

She wrapped her arms around his neck as he bent his head to meet her lips. He tasted of pepperoni, beer and a sweet hot fire that spread heat from her head to her toes.

In the back of her mind she knew this was all wrong, but her body and her response to him screamed that it was all right. One more time, that was all she needed from him.

One more chance to feel his body against hers, one more time to revel in the pleasure she knew he'd give to her. One more time it would be enough because it would have to be enough.

The kiss lasted only moments and then he stepped back from her, took her by the hand and led her down the hallway to the master bedroom.

On the night he'd cleaned up the wound on her head, she'd noticed the black-and-gray spread on the king-size bed, the matching black lamps on the cherry wood end tables and a large dresser.

This time he gave her no opportunity to notice anything as he pulled her back into his arms for a searing kiss. He pulled her so tightly against him that she could feel that he was already fully aroused and that only increased her own desire.

This kiss lingered, was more intimate than the last. Their tongues met and swirled in frantic fervor. His hands stroked up and down her back, as if eager to get beneath the blouse she wore and feel her naked skin.

She ended the kiss and stepped away from him. Evening light filtered through the curtains and lit the room with a romantic golden glow. Her fingers trembled as she began to unbutton her blouse.

By the time she shrugged it off her shoulders, Daniel had already placed his gun belt and cell phone on the nightstand and had his shirt and slacks off. He peeled off his socks, leaving him clad only in a pair of navy boxers.

As Olivia kicked off her shoes and took off her slacks, Daniel pulled the bedspread down, revealing black-and-gray striped sheets.

He got beneath the sheets and watched as she took off her hose, leaving her only in a pair of pale pink panties and a matching lacy bra.

"I can't tell you how many times I've replayed in my mind that night with you in New Orleans," he said, his voice husky and unusually deep.

"I've thought about it, too," she admitted. She got into the bed and he instantly pulled her into his arms. His bare skin was warm against hers and his hands moved to her back and her bra fastening. He had it undone in a mere second. He pulled it off her shoulders and tossed it to the floor as his mouth found hers once again.

His broad chest against her naked breasts provided an exquisite sensation and when his hands moved to cover them, a gasp of pleasure escaped her.

This couldn't be wrong when it felt so right. This couldn't be wrong because she had both eyes open and knew not to expect anything more from him than these moments in his bed.

Another gasp escaped from her as his lips left her mouth and trailed down her neck and then captured the tip of one of her breasts.

She moved her hands to the back of his head, keeping him there as he kissed and sucked. He moved his head just enough to give attention to her other breast, teasing and licking as electric tingles shot through her center and spread to encompass her entire body.

It didn't take long before she wanted them both completely naked. She needed to touch him, to taste him. She wanted him to remember this time with her as she knew she'd always remember it.

She took the lead, breaking away from him and tugging on his boxers. His eyes glowed a silvery green as she finished removing his boxers.

"My turn," he whispered. He slipped his thumbs between the sides of her panties and her bare skin. With agonizing slowness he pulled her panties down her thighs, below her knees and finally off her body.

He slid his hands back up her legs, as if memorizing their shape by touch alone. She ran her hands down his chest, loving the play of his muscles beneath the warm flesh.

He moaned as she wrapped her fingers around his hardness. She moved her hand up and down, stroking him to a higher fever of passion. He tangled his fingers in her hair and moaned her name as she continued to caress him intimately. She leaned down and took him in her mouth, and his fingers tightened their tangle in her tresses.

"You're driving me crazy," he said, his voice distorted with his desire.

She stopped and looked at him. "I want you crazy. I want you insane for me." Once again she began to lick and suck his velvety hardness until he finally pushed her away.

"No more," he panted. "If you don't stop now I'll be done, and I don't want this to be done yet."

"I don't want this done yet, either," she replied.

She hadn't had enough of him yet. The scent of his cologne dizzied her head and she wished she could capture it to have it in her senses forever.

He rolled her over on her back and began to love her body, starting at her lips and then slowly moving downward. It was as if he'd made love to her a hundred times before and knew just where to touch, exactly where to kiss to bring her the most pleasure.

Once again he latched on to one of her swollen nipples and teased and tormented. While his mouth gave special attention to her breasts, one of his hands stroked down her stomach and to the place she most wanted... needed his touch.

She arched her hips to meet him, surprised to find herself close to an explosive release. He knew just the right amount of pressure, just the right speed of finger movement to bring her quickly to the edge where she cascaded over with a violent intensity that left her breathless and weak.

"Again," she managed to gasp as her hands clutched tightly to his shoulders.

He laughed, a low sexy rumble and once again moved his fingers to touch her intimately. This time her climax was less intense but no less pleasurable.

"Now I want you inside me."

"I love a woman who knows exactly what she wants." He moved between her thighs and slowly eased into her. She closed her eyes and gripped him firmly by the shoulders, loving the way they fit so perfectly together.

They moved together in a rhythm her body remembered despite the years that had gone by. They started slow and then increased their pace, and despite the fact that he'd already given her two exquisite climaxes, the crashing waves of yet another one approached.

As if he sensed how close she was, he increased the depth and quickness of his strokes inside her. She once again gasped his name as the waves threatened to drown her and she shuddered uncontrollably.

He thrust a final time into her, moaning her name and finding his own release. He collapsed halfway on top of her, the bulk of his weight held on his elbows. His face was mere inches from hers and he used his hands to brush her hair away from her face. He then kissed her so tenderly it was as if he reached inside her and caressed her heart.

At least she knew tonight wouldn't produce any unintended consequences. She'd been on the pill since after Lily's birth. Thinking about Lily made her realize it was time for her to get home.

"I've got to go," she said.

"Stay," he replied, his voice filled with a soft yearning that tugged at her heart. "Spend tonight with me, Olivia. Just this one night, stay and wake up in my arms in the morning."

She could think of a million reasons why she shouldn't,

one of the biggest because she wanted to so badly. "I really should get home," she replied, and still she didn't make a move to get out of the bed.

"I can get mozzarella sticks delivered to Lily if you'll let her share her mommy with me tonight."

She smiled up at him. "You realize that's blatant manipulation."

"If it works then I'm not apologizing."

Her head said to get up and leave, to go home where she belonged. But for just tonight she wanted to pretend that she belonged here with him.

"Order the cheese sticks. I'm not going anywhere," she said, unaware that she had made up her mind before the words fell out of her mouth.

He rolled over to the side of the bed and picked up his cell phone. While he made the call to Jimmy's Place, she scooted out of bed, grabbed her blouse and pulled it around her. She went down the hallway first to the bathroom and then to the kitchen to retrieve her purse and her own cell phone.

She quickly texted her mother that she was pulling another overnighter and fought the wave of guilt that swept over her. She didn't like to lie to her mother, but what was she supposed to do? Text her that she'd just had hot sex with Daniel and wanted to spend the rest of the night in his arms?

She dropped her phone back into her purse and picked up her gun belt from the floor and carried them both back to the bedroom.

"Mozzarella sticks ordered and will be delivered within fifteen minutes or so," Daniel said.

"And I just texted Mom to let her know I wouldn't be home until morning." She dropped her purse on the floor and placed her gun belt on the nightstand. She then removed her blouse and got back into the bed with him.

He immediately pulled her back into his arms and she placed her head on his chest, where she could hear his steady heartbeat in her ear.

He stroked up and down her back with one hand and a relaxation she hadn't felt since first arriving in Lost Lagoon swept over her.

She'd deal with recriminations and potential regrets tomorrow. Tonight she just wanted to feel like a woman who was loved and cherished. Tonight she just wanted to pretend that she was snuggled against the man who was meant to be in her life forever.

It was a wonderful fantasy that she knew would be shattered by the morning light.

Chapter Ten

There was no question that waking with Olivia in his arms had been wonderful. Throughout the next day, Daniel could think of little else except what they'd shared the night before and then waking to the early morning dawn with her warm naked curves cuddled next to him.

He'd expected the morning to be awkward, and it had been. Olivia had been eager to get back home and shower and change and then get back to the office. She'd been distant but not completely closed off. As they drank coffee they'd made plans for him to eat dinner at her place that evening and then surprise Lily with a trip to the ice cream parlor.

He'd followed her to her house and waited in the driveway while she showered and dressed and then got into her car. He'd then followed her to the station where she'd disappeared into her office.

He knew her time here was running out with just a couple of weeks or so left. She'd been sent here to check the department for any further corruption, and he knew from her conversations with him that she'd pretty well completed her internal investigation.

Solving Shelly's murder had not been the reason she'd been sent here to take over as sheriff. It was very possible, despite the rumor they'd begun of an imminent arrest, that the case would fall on the next sheriff's desk.

It surprised him how much he would miss her when she left. He'd known all along she was only here temporarily, and he'd thought having her in his life, in his bed temporarily would be fine, that it would be enough for him.

But he wasn't ready to tell her goodbye yet. At least he had the evening to look forward to, sharing dinner with Olivia, Rose and Lily, and then surprising Lily with the trip to the ice cream parlor.

"One day at a time," he muttered to himself.

Josh looked up from his desk nearby. "Did you say something?"

"Nothing worthwhile," Daniel replied. He leaned back in his chair and released a deep sigh. "I just thought that something would have happened by now to break the Sinclair case wide open."

"It hasn't been that long since you and Sheriff Bradford put out the word that an arrest was about to happen," Josh replied.

"Yeah, but I thought once word got out, the murderer would panic and do something stupid or at least do something that would bring him into our awareness. So far all of our suspects are going about their lives as usual."

"Which begs the question of do we even have the perp on our list of suspects?" Josh replied.

"Bite your tongue," Daniel said. "I don't even want to think about the possibility that there's somebody out there we don't know about, somebody who has managed to stay out of our radar for all this time."

"If you think about it, Shelly could have been murdered by almost any man in town," Josh continued. "I mean, she was a pretty young woman sitting on a bench in an isolated part of town in the middle of the night."

"All the people we have on our suspect list have potential motive in her murder. Why would a man who just happened upon her murder her?" Daniel's frustration grew by the minute.

"I'm just throwing out suppositions. Her diamond ring was stolen. Maybe it was nothing more than somebody needing the money to pawn the ring. Or, maybe it was a potential sexual assault gone bad."

"Her purse was left on the bench and she had both cash and a credit card inside that wasn't stolen. It wasn't a robbery and you're really going out of your way to ruin my day," Daniel replied.

Josh grinned at him. "That's what good friends are for."

Daniel returned his attention to the file in front of him. He'd already considered all the scenarios Josh had brought up. It was possible the guilty person wasn't on their suspect list, but his gut instinct told him he was.

Shelly's engagement ring had been pretty, but certainly not a large diamond that could be pawned for any sizable amount of money. Besides, they'd contacted every pawn shop in the state to let them know about the stolen ring.

To the best of everyone's knowledge, the ring hadn't been pawned. Also Shelly's clothing hadn't shown any indication of a sexual attack. No rips or tears, nothing to point to a potential molestation.

At noon he stuck his head into Olivia's office to see if she wanted to go out for a bite to eat, but she declined, telling him that she intended to work through lunch.

Instead of eating out, Josh drove through George's Diner and picked up burgers and fries and the two deputies went into the small break room to eat lunch.

"I don't want to eat too much," Josh said as he unwrapped one of the smaller burgers George offered on his menu. "Savannah is making beef Wellington for dinner tonight."

"When are you going to marry that girl?"

Josh smiled and his eyes softened. "Actually, we're planning a small ceremony and a reception in two months. Savannah has had her head in bridal magazines and she's planning on doing most of the work herself. I'm actually glad you brought it up because I've been meaning to ask you if you'd be my best man."

Daniel swallowed his bite of burger and chased it with a quick sip of his soda, surprised and touched by Josh's question. "I'd be honored to be your best man," he replied.

"Good, I was hoping you'd agree."

"I know Savannah had always wanted to open a fine-dining restaurant here in town. Has she given up on that idea?"

"Not at all," Josh said. "She gave up on the idea when Shelly was murdered. She gave up on pretty much everything then, but she now intends to follow through on that dream after our wedding."

"And what do you think about that?"

Josh smiled, again a softness creeping into his eyes. "I want her to fulfill every dream she'll ever have. I totally support the idea of her opening a restaurant. Besides, it would be great if she got it up and running at around the same time that the theme park opens. Tourists will flock to a nice restaurant while they're on vacation."

"Sounds like a good plan," Daniel agreed and then frowned. "And now if only we had a good plan to get this murder case solved and filed away forever."

Daniel spent the rest of the afternoon reading through all of the interviews they had conducted, trying to glean a new name, another piece of information that might move their investigation forward.

By five o'clock he was more than ready to call it a day and enjoy dinner with Olivia and her family. "It's a perfect ice cream evening," he said as he and Olivia left by the back door and stepped into the humid, hot air.

"Lily is going to be so excited. She and my mom have been cooped up in that house since the day we arrived in town."

He was pleased that the distance he'd felt radiating

from her that morning was gone and everything appeared normal between them.

"I'll see you at your house," he said as they reached her car. He waited for her to get inside her vehicle and then hurried to his own so that he could follow her.

As he drove he tried to empty his mind of all thoughts about murder and about Olivia's assignment here being over soon. He just wanted to enjoy every minute of time with her that he could before it was time for her to move on.

It didn't take long for the two of them to park in front of the bright yellow shanty she called home for now. Lily's pixie face was pressed against the front window and lit with joy at the sight of them approaching the door.

"Nanny, they're here!" Her voice drifted out and Daniel couldn't help the smile that curved his lips at the sound of her excitement. Somehow the little minx had managed to capture a little piece of his heart.

Olivia opened the door and immediately moved to the pad on the wall to deal with the alarm. Meanwhile Lily grabbed Daniel's hand and smiled up at him.

"Nanny told me you were eating with us again tonight and I was so happy," she exclaimed.

"I was happy, too. I'd much rather eat Nanny's cooking than my own," Daniel replied.

"Do you cook bad?" Lily asked.

"I don't cook very good," Daniel replied.

"We're having my favorite, meat loaf and Nanny's homemade mac and cheese," Lily said.

"How about a hello for your mother?" Olivia asked as she unfastened her gun belt and placed it in its usual spot on the top of one of the kitchen cabinets.

"Hello, Mommy." Lily dropped Daniel's hand and rushed toward her mother for a round of kisses and hugs.

"Good evening, Deputy Carson," Rose said with a warm smile.

"Same to you and please make it Daniel."

"Then Daniel it is," she replied with a pleased expression.

"Now, what can I do to help?"

Olivia and Lily had disappeared into Rose's bedroom where he knew Olivia would be changing clothes.

"Absolutely nothing. Just sit and relax. How about a tall glass of lemonade?"

"That sounds great," he agreed and sat at the table in the chair where he had sat each time he'd shared a meal with them.

Rose poured him a glass of the cold beverage and while they waited for Olivia and Lily to return from the bedroom, he and Rose chatted about the pirate theme park that would eventually open.

"It will definitely change things around here," he said. "With all the tourists they're hoping to attract the town will benefit both financially and socially."

"We haven't had a chance to really see any of the town," Rose said as she pulled a large meat loaf from the lower rack of the oven. "Olivia has insisted we stay inside and don't go exploring. I even have groceries delivered here."

"Maybe we can change that a little bit this evening," Olivia said as she and Lily returned to the room. She looked positively stunning with her hair loose around her shoulders and clad in white shorts and a sleeveless hot-pink blouse. Lily was like a mini-me in pink shorts and a pink-and-white checked top. Daniel got back to his feet at the sight of them.

"Change it how?" Rose asked curiously.

"Daniel and I have a little surprise planned for after dinner," Olivia replied.

"A surprise? Tell me, Mommy. Tell me the surprise." Lily jumped up and down.

Olivia laughed and shook her head. "Nope. My lips are sealed. It won't be a surprise if I tell you now."

Lily immediately turned her attention to Daniel. She sidled up next to him and gazed up at him with innocent green eyes that could melt the hardest of hearts.

"Deputy, you can tell me the secret," she said in the sweetest of voices. "It's okay. You can whisper it in my ear."

He laughed and also shook his head. "No way, my little peanut. Your mother would kill me. Besides, if you just be patient and eat a good dinner, then it will be time for the secret and you'll know it."

Lily heaved a dramatic sigh. "Nanny, is it time to eat? We have to eat fast tonight."

"I'll have it on the table in just a jiffy," Rose replied. "Everyone go ahead and sit while I finish things up."

The three of them sat as Rose sliced the meat loaf and set a platter in the center of the table. She added a big bowl of green beans and a large crock dish of creamy-looking mac and cheese.

The food was delicious, but it was the company that filled Daniel's soul and made him realize just how much he was going to miss not only Olivia, but her family as well when they all returned to their life in Natchez.

"I'll tell you the secret once the kitchen is all cleaned," Olivia said as they finished eating.

Rose had never had so much help clearing dishes from the table and loading the dishwasher. Both Lily and Daniel scrambled to finish the cleanup in record time.

Olivia fought a burst of giggles as the two of them bumped into each other several times in their haste to finish up. Finally the work was done and Lily climbed up on Olivia's lap and placed her hands on either side of her mother's face.

"It's time for the secret," she said.

"Okay. Daniel and I thought it would be nice if we'd all take a trip into town to an ice cream parlor," Olivia said.

Lily's eyes widened and she clapped her hands together and quickly scampered off Olivia's lap. "That's a great surprise. So, let's go!"

It took several minutes for them to actually get out the door. Rose went into her bedroom to freshen up and grab her purse, and Olivia grabbed her gun belt and pulled her gun from her holster and placed it in her purse.

It was a grim reminder that this wasn't just a simple social outing without the potential for danger. Danger could come at them wearing any face, cloaked in any body shape and size. She only hoped she wasn't putting her two most precious people in her life at risk. She hoped Daniel was right when he'd doubted that the perp would make a move on her in a public place. Surely he wouldn't want any witnesses around.

Besides, between her and Daniel they could manage to have an ice cream parlor experience without trouble. She didn't even want to think about last night, when she'd slept in his arms and wished on a star that things could be different.

She didn't want to focus on how neatly he fit into her little family without any ripples. Rose and Lily both adored him, and he appeared to be as taken with them. Fantasy. She couldn't dwell in fantasies.

Daniel drove with Olivia riding shotgun and Rose and Lily in the backseat. As he hit Main Street, he pointed out stores and other places he thought would interest Rose and Lily.

Rose was particularly interested in Mama Baptiste's shop when Daniel told her Mama sold all kinds of herbs and spices in addition to her secret rubs and potions for ailments.

He also pointed out The Pirate's Inn, but instead of talking about ghosts and hauntings that might have scared Lily, he talked about the pirates who had once used Lost Lagoon as a land base.

Charlie's Ice Cream Parlor was located across the

street from Jimmy's Place and was a throwback to the past with pink-and-white umbrella tables dotting a patio area in front and a matching awning.

Several couples were seated at the tables as Olivia, Daniel, Rose and Lily went inside to get their cold goodies. Charlie Berk, proud owner of the place, introduced himself. He stood behind a refrigerated counter that appeared to stretch forever.

Round barrels of various flavors of ice cream were tucked inside the glass-topped counter, and on top of the counter were a variety of syrups, sprinkles and other candies to add to the sinfulness of the ice cream. The syrups were controlled by Charlie, but the sprinkles and candy containers held scoopers for customers to help themselves.

"Sprinkles!" Lily exclaimed in delight. "I love sprinkles!"

"I'm thinking a banana split sounds good," Daniel said.

"And I'm thinking a waffle cone of peanut butter ice cream with chocolate chips on top," Olivia said.

"And I'm still thinking," Rose replied as she walked up and down the counter as if overwhelmed by the many choices.

"What about you, munchkin?" Daniel asked Lily. Olivia already knew what her daughter's answer would be.

"A waffle cone with chocolate ice cream and lots and lots of sprinkles," Lily replied.

Rose finally decided on a bowl of strawberry shortcake ice cream with fresh strawberries and whipped cream topping. Orders were placed and delivered and then the four of them moved outside to one of the empty umbrella tables.

Once again Olivia was struck by the fact that they looked like the perfect family. She and Daniel had made sweet love the night before and shared dinner together and now they had their daughter and Olivia's mother out for ice cream.

What would happen if she told Daniel the truth? He talked the talk of a confirmed bachelor, but his actions said otherwise. It was obvious he was quite charmed by Lily. Would he really be so horrified to discover that he was Lily's father? Would he be angry that she hadn't told him before?

Despite the fact that she'd lain in his arms the night before and he was laughing at Lily's antics as she tried to capture the drips of her quickly melting cone, he had given her no indication that he wanted anything with her expect what they now shared…a temporary relationship while she was here.

He hadn't awakened this morning after making such passionate love with her last night and suddenly spouted words of everlasting love for her.

Nothing had really changed to make her believe he would welcome the news that he had a daughter. In the end, it was a secret she knew she wouldn't divulge to him.

For all intents and purposes, her husband, Phil, had been Lily's father. He had changed her diapers and walked the floors with her when she'd been colicky in the middle of the night. He was the man who had celebrated her first step and her first word.

Unfortunately, Lily had few memories of the big man with the big heart who had married Olivia because he'd loved her desperately and wanted to take care of her and her unborn child.

They were almost finished with their treats when she saw Jimmy Tambor approaching from across the street. "Hey, guys," he said with a friendly smile as he spied them at their table and paused.

"Hi, Jimmy. Aren't you in the middle of dinner rush?" Daniel asked.

Jimmy waved a hand dismissively. "Yeah, but they can handle if for a while without me. I had a craving for Charlie's raspberry chocolate chip ice cream and decided to sneak away for a few minutes. I've got great staff and things run pretty much on their own, so nobody really misses me when I'm gone."

He crouched down next to Lily. "And you must be the little girl who likes my mozzarella sticks."

Lily's eyes widened. "You make them?"

"I sure do," Jimmy replied.

"I love them, almost as much as ice cream," Lily replied.

Jimmy laughed and straightened up. "I haven't heard any more about the investigation. Things still on track for an arrest?"

"We're just crossing our t's and dotting our i's," Olivia replied. How she wished that was the case. She was be-

ginning to believe that the murder wouldn't be solved before she'd be called back to Natchez. She'd spent most of
the day putting her last touches on the report she would
send to the attorney general about her internal investigation.

"Well, enjoy the last of your ice cream," Jimmy said
and then with another of his friendly smiles he left their
table and disappeared into the shop.

Olivia watched him go, her brain suddenly firing off
in all directions. Jimmy Tambor hadn't made the list of
suspects and yet he'd been here at the time of the murder. He had probably had a close relationship to Shelly
because of his close friendship with Bo.

The steak knife that had been found next to her when
she'd been attacked in the station parking lot had come
from the restaurant he pretended to own, and he seemed
particularly interested in keeping track of where they
were in the investigation.

"Earth to Olivia." Daniel's deep voice brought her
back to the here and now.

Lily giggled. "Earth to Mommy," she repeated.

"I'm here. Sorry, I just got lost in my head for a minute," she replied. Surely, she was just grasping at desperate straws in even considering Jimmy as a suspect.

"I asked if we were ready to go," Daniel said.

"Ready," she replied. They got up from the table and
she made sure all the napkins were placed in the nearby
trash receptacle and then they were back in Daniel's car
and headed back to the house.

"We should have surprises more often," Lily said. "Like maybe every day."

Daniel laughed and Olivia watched him shoot an affectionate glance into his rearview mirror. "If you had a surprise every day then they wouldn't be special anymore. Personally, I think this surprise was very special."

"Me, too," Lily replied. "And I'm 'specially happy that you got to eat ice cream with us, Deputy."

By that time they were home. As Rose and Lily headed inside, Olivia touched Daniel's arm and lingered on the front porch. "Thanks for the great idea. It's been fun."

"It has been fun," he agreed. "But you seemed a bit distracted there for a few minutes."

"Jimmy distracted me. I found myself wondering why he isn't a serious suspect on our list."

Daniel frowned. "I guess he didn't make the short list because he and Bo have always been so close. It's hard to believe he'd have anything to do with killing his best friend's girlfriend."

"Do you remember where he was on the night of Shelly's murder?" she asked.

"I'd have to look back in the files to be sure, but I think he was working at Bo's Place that night," he replied.

"I'd like to double-check that again and maybe have another chat with Bo tomorrow," she said thoughtfully. "I don't know, maybe I'm crazy, but no stone left unturned, right?"

"Okay, whatever you want," he agreed. He held her

gaze for a long moment. "Do we need to talk about last night?"

Heat instantly fired in her cheeks. "The only thing to talk about is the fact that it shouldn't happen again. It won't happen again," she corrected herself.

"But I already want it to." He reached out and ran his fingers through a strand of her hair, then caressed his fingers down the side of her face.

She stepped away from him. Damn him. His very touch set off a yearning inside her that she had to ignore, that she somehow had to cast out.

"Daniel, I can't make love to you again because I refuse to leave here with my heart broken. We don't want the same things from life. We're wrong for each other on so many levels, and yet I've allowed myself to get emotionally involved with you and it has to stop now."

A hint of surprise shone from his eyes and then was gone. He released a deep sigh and raked a hand through his hair. "You're almost finished here, aren't you?"

She nodded. "I finished the report on the internal investigation today. Once I send it in, it should just be a matter of days before a special election is set and once a new sheriff is elected, I'll for sure be gone."

A hollowness filled her at her own words. If things were different she wouldn't have minded calling Lost Lagoon home. If Daniel loved her, if he wanted a family… but that was her fantasy and not his.

"The most important thing now is that we close out the Sinclair case before I leave," she continued, desperately needing to get the conversation back on a professional level.

"Then we go to talk to Bo in the morning and see what he can tell us about his friend, Jimmy." His green eyes were darker than usual and impossible to read.

"Good. I'll be ready to get to the office by seven," she said.

He nodded. "Then I'll be out here around that time to follow you in."

She placed a hand on his arm, unable to stop herself. "Thank you for tonight and for everything you've done to support and protect me." She dropped her arm back to her side. "But we need to keep things strictly professional from here on out." Her heart clenched. "I don't want you getting any closer to my family, especially Lily. It will just make it harder for her, for all of us, when we leave here."

"Olivia, it sounds like you're telling me goodbye and you aren't leaving yet."

"I just wanted you to understand that last night was a one-time thing that won't be repeated."

"Message received," he replied, his eyes still darker than usual. "And on that note I'll just say good-night and I'll see you in the morning."

She watched from the porch as he walked to his car, got inside and then finally disappeared from her sight. What he didn't realize was that she had been saying goodbye...goodbye to any fantasy she might have entertained about them all becoming a family. A farewell to any dreams she might have entertained about him becoming more than just the biological father to Lily.

She was in love with him and more than anything, she had to say goodbye to that particular emotion.

Chapter Eleven

The ice cream session definitely hadn't ended the way Daniel had imagined. He wasn't sure what he'd expected, but it hadn't been her confessing to him that she'd become emotionally involved with him and giving him a premature goodbye.

The next morning as he sat outside her house waiting for her to emerge, he played and replayed their conversation in his head.

She'd said she didn't want to leave here with a broken heart, which implied she was falling in love with him. It was probably good that she'd put a brake on things, because he was getting way too into her and the company of her family.

Footloose and fancy-free, that was how he'd always envisioned himself. He'd never wanted to make the same mistakes his parents had made. He had never wanted the ugliness he'd lived through when they had divorced.

But he had become increasingly aware in the last couple of months of how love had added richness to the lives of those around him and that what he'd gone through in his childhood was caused by two selfish, dysfunctional people.

For the past couple of days he'd been at war with himself, discovering that his attraction to Olivia was far deeper than mere lust and yet afraid of changing his chosen solitary path through life.

He was thirty-three years old and since the time that he was eighteen, he'd opted for comfort and ease. He didn't need or want anyone in his life on a permanent basis. He was happy being alone, he told himself.

He breathed a sigh of relief as she appeared on the porch and pulled him from his troubling thoughts. She was all business today, with her hair pulled back in a grim bun and clad in the khaki uniform of her station.

She gave him a small wave and then got into her car. He followed her to the station where they both parked and he fell into step next to her as they headed for the building.

"Sleep well?" he asked.

"To be honest, I didn't sleep well," she replied.

"That futon can't be the most comfortable place to sleep."

"It's not, but I couldn't find a three-bedroom place to rent when we needed to be here. Besides, it wasn't the futon that kept me tossing and turning all night. Shelly's murder has a hold on me like few cases I've ever worked in the past."

"Trust me, it's been a stab in my heart every time it's crossed my mind. I just wish we could have done a complete investigation when it happened."

"Your hands were tied by your boss."

"Yeah, but I should have done more." He opened the back door that led into the building and followed behind her inside.

"You're doing the best you can now, and hopefully Bo will give us some information about Jimmy Tambor to get him out of my head as a potential suspect." She frowned. "I know my job here wasn't to solve murder cases, but I'd really like to close this one out before I'm called back to Natchez."

They entered the squad room where several of the other deputies sat at their desks. "What time are we going to talk to Bo?"

"I'm going to call him and see if he's available around ten. I'll let you know what I set up with him." With a curt nod of dismissal, she entered her office and closed the door behind her.

Cool and professional, she was definitely setting a new tone between them. He'd follow her lead because he didn't want to make things difficult for her. He cared about her too much to pursue a deeper relationship with her that would only create pain and heartache for her and for sweet Lily when they left.

He sat at his desk and checked the notes left by James Rockfield, the deputy who worked the shift before him. Just because he and the small task force had been focused on solving Shelly's murder didn't mean that all other crime in town had stopped.

There had been a smash and grab at the liquor store on Main Street. The culprit had gotten away with several bottles of booze and three cartons of cigarettes. The owner had called a glass company to replace the broken front window and the security camera had captured old man Clyde Dorfman in the act. Unfortunately, James and the night crew had been unable to locate Clyde to make an arrest.

Daniel picked up the report and carried it to Ray McClure's desk. Ray sat sipping coffee and reading a sports magazine. "Take care of this," Daniel said. "I've got interviews to conduct with the sheriff."

Ray read over the report and then frowned. "How in the hell am I supposed to find Clyde if the night crew couldn't find him? They say right here he wasn't at home when they checked."

"My guess would be that he's probably drunk as a skunk and hiding out in one of the abandoned shanties. Eventually he'll sober up and head home, but in the meantime you might catch him in one of the shanties."

"How could he be so stupid? He had to have known there was a security camera."

"Clyde has never been the brightest bulb in the pack and he was probably already half-drunk when he committed the crime," Daniel replied.

Ray pulled himself out of his chair. "That man spends more time in jail sobering up than he does in that dive where he lives."

"This time if charges are pressed, he'll spend a lot more time in jail," Daniel replied. "This isn't going to be a simple drunk-and-disorderly charge."

He waited until Ray had disappeared out of the back door before he returned to his desk. Although he knew he should be thinking about the interview they would soon be conducting with Bo, his thoughts wandered back to Olivia and how much fun it had been sharing ice cream with her family the night before, how much he enjoyed eating dinner with them and how easily he'd fit into her personal life.

She was no longer simply Lily, the striking woman he'd picked up in a bar and had shared a fantasy night of lovemaking. She was Olivia, intelligent and strong and a loving mother and daughter.

It was just before nine when she stuck her head out the door and told him she'd set up to meet Bo and Claire at their house at ten.

Personally, Daniel thought the whole thing was just a wild-goose chase. The idea of Jimmy Tambor being a murderer seemed as far-fetched as alcoholic Clyde ever putting down the bottle.

At nine forty-five he and Olivia left the station to head to Bo and Claire's place. Olivia was quiet as they got into his car.

"Are you still going to be my friend?" he asked only half-seriously as he started the car.

She turned and looked at him first in surprise, and then smiled when she realized he was teasing her. "I have to keep you as a friend. You're the only one I have in town. I just can't be your friend with benefits."

"And I'll respect that," he replied. He didn't want to respect it. He didn't have to like it. He wanted her again…and again. But he knew, in the depths of his heart, she was right in her decision.

She was a woman looking for something different in

her life. Having a short affair with him wouldn't give her what she wanted...what she needed. She had told him she wanted to marry again and give Lily a father to love. He just wasn't that man.

When they reached Bo and Claire's place, Bo greeted them at the front door and ushered them inside where the four of them sat at the table.

"I've heard through the grapevine that you're rebuilding on your mother's property where the house burned down," Daniel said. Bo's childhood home had been burned down by Claire's stalker, who was now in jail.

"The contractor is just getting started, but we're hoping that within about three months or so we'll have a new home to move into," Bo said. He glanced at Claire and the love in his eyes was unmistakable. "This house has been great, but it's way too little for a family and we're both ready to start having children."

Claire smiled. "And we both want at least a couple of kids."

"You won't regret it," Olivia said. "Having my daughter was the best thing I ever did in my life."

"But I'm sure you aren't here to talk about new houses and parenthood," Bo said.

"We want to ask you some questions about Jimmy Tambor," Olivia said.

"Jimmy?" Bo looked at her in surprise. "What about him?"

"I understand you two have been friends for a long time," Olivia said.

"Jimmy and I have been like brothers since we were in grade school. He had a brutal, abusive father and an absent mother and we sort of took him in. Most nights Jimmy ate dinner with us, and during the summers he spent most of his time at our house. He was always a bit smaller than me so my mother gave him my hand-me-down clothes and treated him like a son."

"And your friendship remained strong as you grew older?" Olivia asked.

Bo nodded. "Definitely. When I opened Bo's Place, I gave Jimmy a job there and he moved into an upstairs apartment with me."

"How did he get along with Shelly?" Daniel asked.

Bo's eyes narrowed slightly. "Where are you going with this? Surely you don't believe Jimmy had anything to do with Shelly's death? He cared about Shelly. The three of us got along great. Besides, from what I heard you had a suspect ready to arrest."

"We're just tying up some loose ends, and we realized Jimmy hadn't really been investigated at the time of the murder."

Bo released a dry, slightly irritated laugh. "That's because there was no real investigation at the time of the murder. Trey Walker pointed a finger of blame squarely on me and never did anything to find anyone else who might have been responsible."

"And we're trying to rectify that," Olivia said.

"If you're seriously looking at Jimmy as a suspect, then you're dredging the bottom of the swamp. When I left town under the weight of all the suspicion, Jimmy moved in with my mother to help take care of her. He took over my business to keep it running. He's always been there when I needed him. He would never do anything to hurt me, and he knew more than anyone how much I loved Shelly."

Bo paused and released a ragged sigh as he looked first at Daniel and then at Olivia. "You're no closer to finding out who killed Shelly than Trey Walker was." It wasn't a question. It was a statement that shot a new pang of guilt through Daniel.

Olivia's features reflected not only the guilt Daniel felt, but also the painful knowledge that Bo was right.

"Surely, if there was something strange going on between Jimmy and Shelly, Bo would have sensed it," Olivia said a few minutes later when they were back in Daniel's car.

"He seemed adamant that Jimmy didn't have anything to do with Shelly's death," Daniel replied. "Bo knows Jimmy better than anyone in town."

"Does Jimmy have a girlfriend? Did he have one when Shelly was murdered?"

Daniel cast her a quick glance and frowned as he focused back on the road. "You know, now that I think about it, I can't remember any woman that Jimmy has ever dated, although that doesn't mean he hasn't had girlfriends. I never paid much attention to him, except to meet and greet when I go to Jimmy's Place for a meal."

Olivia frowned and stared out the passenger window. Who had killed Shelly Sinclair? They had no concrete evidence to point to anyone specifically. Their ruse of putting out the word that an arrest was about to happen hadn't done anything.

She didn't know what else to do to solve the crime. Bo was right, they were no closer to catching the killer than Trey Walker had been when he'd been sheriff.

"Your frustration is alive and well and filling the car," Daniel said, breaking into her troubled thoughts.

"Sorry, I can't help it. I really hoped to clear this case."

"We still have some time," he replied.

"Some time, but we don't have any more leads."

"Something will pop," he said confidently as he pulled into a parking space behind the sheriff's building. He shut off the car and turned to look at her. "We have to stay positive, Olivia. That's what makes us good lawmen—we don't stop. We don't give up."

She gazed at his handsome countenance and almost regretted her decision to halt all physical contact between them. She didn't just lust after him. Being in his arms had made her feel safe and completely feminine. He'd tapped into the woman inside her, beyond the tough cloak she wore as a strong and competent sheriff.

"Are you planning on running for sheriff when they hold the special election?" she asked, trying to forget that she'd ever experienced the wonder of being held in his arms, of being kissed so passionately.

He laughed and shook his head. "No way. In fact, I've been offered another job that I'm seriously considering. Rod Nixon called me a couple of days ago and asked if I'd be interested in heading up the security team for the amusement park."

She looked at him in surprise. "You could just walk away from your badge?"

"I don't know," he admitted. "That's why I told Rod I'd need some time to consider it. To be honest, working with a man like Trey kind of soured me for the job."

"You're good at what you do," she replied, still stunned by what he'd said about walking away from law enforcement.

"I'd be just as good at running security at the park," he countered. "Come on, let's get inside. I feel like I'm baking out here."

A few minutes later, Olivia was back in her office and Daniel was at his desk. Her blinds were open so she could see into the squad room.

Again and again her gaze was drawn to Daniel, who was on his laptop probably working up a report of their conversation with Bo.

She loved him. She was in love with him and there was nothing she could do about it. She would leave Lost Lagoon with a wounded heart that would eventually scar, but she'd never be able to forget Deputy Daniel Carson.

Each time she looked into Lily's green eyes, she would remember the man who was the girl's father. She would mourn the fact that he had no desire to have a wife or children. He simply wasn't a family man.

It was particularly cruel of fate to bring her here with him, knowing that he could never be the man in her life. It had been particularly stupid of her to allow him so far into her heart, to allow him to be a part of her family for even a brief moment.

It was noon when Daniel opened her door and asked her if she wanted to go someplace for lunch. She declined and told him she would just order in something from Jimmy's Place.

A half an hour later, a teenager delivered a chicken Caesar salad to her and as she ate she tried to keep her mind empty.

She needed a little mental break from the Sinclair case and from thoughts of Daniel. Instead she allowed her mind to dwell on Lily and her mother. Despite the fact that Lily had been unplanned, she'd been a gift from God, completing Olivia's life in a way she'd never dreamed possible.

Rose's support had also been a godsend. Only she knew that Lily hadn't been Phil's child, but rather the result of a one-night stand. Of course Rose had no idea that the one-night stand had been with Daniel.

Even though Rose hadn't approved of her daughter's risky behavior that night so long ago, she'd stood by Olivia throughout her pregnancy and after.

Sooner than later, the three of them would return to their apartment in Natchez and resume the life they had led before coming to Lost Lagoon.

They had been fine without Daniel before and they would continue to be fine when they got back home. Nothing had really changed.

After lunch she called Ray McClure into her office. He updated her on the liquor store break-in, reporting that Clyde still hadn't made an appearance anywhere to make an arrest.

"Then what are you doing sitting in the squad room?" Olivia asked. "Why aren't you out on the streets still looking for him?"

"I got hot and decided to come in for a little while," Ray replied, his voice half-whiny.

"We sometimes have to work in uncomfortable situations. It's part of your job." Olivia straightened in her chair and stared hard at Ray, who finally broke the gaze and looked down at the floor.

"Ray, I've finished up my internal investigation here," she continued. He looked at her again, appearing to hold his breath. "Don't worry. I don't believe you had anything to do with the corruption that took place here with the drug operation. But I do believe that you're lazy and a weak link in the department. I'm recommending that you be placed on probation for six months, and if you don't step up by then you won't have a job here any longer. If you do step up, then the probation will be washed clean from your record."

She expected a protest. She fully anticipated a fit of anger from Ray. Instead he released a deep sigh and frowned thoughtfully. "It was easy to be lazy when Trey was in charge. I followed him around and laughed at his stupid jokes and told him how great he was. That was all he expected from me."

"Trey is in jail and things have changed," Olivia replied.

Ray nodded. There was no surly expression, no hint

of insubordination as he straightened in his chair. "All of my life I wanted to work in law enforcement. I lost my drive, gave up my ambition to Trey. It *is* time for a change. I need to get back to the man I was before Trey was boss, and I promise you'll see a different man from now on."

Olivia nodded and noticed that as Ray left the office there was a new confidence in his gait, a determination in the set of his shoulders.

She was pleased with the way things had gone with the deputy. Her instinct was that he'd just been waiting for somebody to call him on the rug, to give him a reason to step up. He'd been allowed to fall into bad habits, but she believed he'd taken her words to heart.

She spent most of the rest of the afternoon rereading the report she intended to email to the attorney general. It had been ready to go for a couple of days, but she'd put off actually sending it, knowing that it would signal the beginning of the end of her time here.

By four o'clock she realized dark clouds had moved in, portending another storm brought on by the heat and humidity of the day and hurricane Dennis that was spinning its strength along the coast.

She'd called a meeting of the task force at four thirty and by the time she made it to the small conference room, all of the lights in the building had been turned on to ward off the darkness outside.

She was disappointed, but not surprised, that none of the task force team members had anything new to add on the Sinclair case.

She was about to dismiss them all when her cell phone rang and she saw from the caller ID that it was Bo McBride. "Bo?"

"It's Jimmy," he said, his voice frantic. "He killed Shelly. After our talk this morning, I decided to go to the bar and I searched his apartment. I found Shelly's ring stuffed in a sock in his drawer." The words tumbled over themselves, fast and furious. "He walked in and I confronted him."

"Where is he now?" Olivia asked urgently.

"He ran down the stairs and just took off in his car, a blue Camry."

"We'll take it from here," Olivia said and disconnected the call. "Jimmy Tambor is Shelly's killer and he just left Jimmy's Place in a blue Camry. Josh, get men and roadblocks set up on every road coming in and out of town. Get everyone out there looking for him. I don't want him getting out of Lost Lagoon."

The men jumped to their feet and left the room. Daniel looked at Olivia. "Come on, you can ride with me," he said.

"If he had Shelly's ring, he has to be the killer," she said. "I wonder why he'd kill her?"

"We don't need to know the why right now. We just have to find him before he gets out of town," Daniel replied as they hurried toward the exit to the parking lot.

They had just gotten into Daniel's car when Olivia's cell phone rang again. It was Deputy Wes Stiller. She punched it on speaker to answer.

"Sheriff Bradford, I found Jimmy's car," he said.

"Where?" Olivia asked, her heart pounding with adrenaline.

"It's parked in front of your house. Luckily, I spotted it while out on patrol in your area. The car is vacant. I think he's inside."

Olivia's breath whooshed out of her as if she'd been sucker punched. Terror ripped through her as Daniel tore out of the parking lot and headed for her house where a killer was now holed up inside with her mother and her daughter.

Chapter Twelve

Daniel drove like a bat out of hell, his heart beating a thousand miles an hour. Still, he knew his heartbeat couldn't be as fast, as frantic as Olivia's.

She sat straight in the seat, her lovely features taut and ashen with the fear he knew must be tearing through her. There was nothing more dangerous than a trapped killer, especially one who had two hostages in his grasp.

"Why would my mother let him inside? She's never met Jimmy before. Why would she unarm the alarm to let him in?" Her voice was soft, and he knew she didn't expect him to have the answers. He wasn't even sure she was aware that she was talking out loud.

They didn't know if he'd gone in armed. Did he have a gun? Or had he left the restaurant with one of his wickedly sharp steak knives? Even if he hadn't, there were plenty of knives inside the house that he could use to hurt either Rose or Lily.

Daniel's heart clenched tight as he thought of the little girl with the bright green eyes and loving nature. And what about sweet, naïve Rose? She certainly had no tools to know how to deal with a desperate man.

Jimmy couldn't have chosen better if he wanted vulnerable hostages.

Lightning flashed and thunder boomed in the distance as they pulled along the side of the road two houses away from Olivia's house. Jimmy's car was parked in front of her place and several patrol cars were parked on either side of the road some distance back.

It was obvious nobody had approached the house and everyone was awaiting Olivia's orders. Her fingers trembled as she unfastened her seat belt. He worried that her legs might not hold her when she opened the door to get out of the car.

She surprised him, getting out and standing tall, none of the fear he'd seen on her face in the car now present as Deputy Wes Stiller approached.

"We need to establish contact," Olivia said. "And I need to know that the two hostages are okay." Her voice broke slightly.

Daniel moved closer to her, fighting the impulse to pull her against his chest, to hold her tight and tell her that everything was going to be all right.

However, he couldn't tell her that everything was going to be okay, nor did he want to undermine her authority in front of the other men. She was the boss and she would call the shots.

"I'll try my mother's cell phone," she said. She punched in the numbers and waited. Daniel stood close enough to her that he could hear it ring over and over again until an answering machine came on. Olivia waited for the beep, and then spoke. "Jimmy, we need to talk. Answer the phone." There was no reply and the call disconnected.

By that time Bo had arrived on scene. He hurried over to Olivia and Daniel as the dark of the storm grew deeper and the lightning got closer.

"I've tried to call him, but he isn't answering any of my calls," Bo said. "I can't believe this is happening. I don't understand any of it. Why would Jimmy do something like this?"

"I don't give a damn why," Olivia snapped. "We just need to get him out of that house and away from my family." Tears filled her eyes and she looked desperately at Daniel. "I need to think like a cop, but right now all I can do is think like a mother."

Daniel looked at Wes. "Get a perimeter of men surrounding the house, but don't get close enough that Jimmy feels more threatened. Just make sure he doesn't escape out the back door."

"Got it," Wes replied and hurried toward the gathering group of officers who had arrived on scene.

Olivia called her mother again, quickly hitting speaker as the call was answered by Rose. "Olivia. He fooled me." Rose's voice trembled with suppressed terror and then she began to cry. "He said he was delivering mozzarella sticks and he had a bag from Jimmy's Place and so I let him in. I'm sorry. I'm so sorry."

"Mom, none of that matters now. I know you're scared. Is Lily okay? Are you both unharmed?" Olivia asked. Her fingers around her cell phone were bone white with tension.

"We're fine, but…" Rose's voice cut out and instead Jimmy's filled the line.

"They're fine for now, but I can't promise you it's going to stay that way," he said.

"Tell me what you want, Jimmy." Olivia's voice was once again strong and controlled. "Tell me how we can resolve this so that nobody gets hurt."

"I'll let you know what I want later." With those words, Jimmy cut the line off. Olivia immediately called back but the phone rang once and then was hung up.

"Let me try again," Bo said. He dialed Jimmy's cell phone number and punched his phone on speaker. To everyone's surprise, Jimmy answered.

"I've got nothing to say to you," Jimmy said.

"Jimmy, just give yourself up. Come out of the house and nobody will get hurt," Bo said.

"I'll go to prison. That bitch of a girlfriend of yours double-crossed me." A wealth of venom deepened Jimmy's voice.

"What are you talking about?" Bo asked in obvious confusion. "Jimmy, I'm begging you as a friend to come out and end this."

"You aren't my friend," Jimmy yelled. "You never were my friend. I was your charity case. You were the golden boy and I got your leftovers. People were only friends with me because of you. The best thing that ever happened to me was when you left town and I got to live your life. I got to live with your mother and run your business."

"What did you do to Shelly?" Bo asked.

"I took her from you. I courted her, and we had plans to leave town together, but on the night it was supposed to happen, she decided she couldn't leave you. You always won. That night I made sure you didn't win. I took her away from you forever."

Jimmy hung up and Bo stared at Daniel in confused horror. "All this time I thought we were friends, and he's hated me."

"I think we just got to the bottom of Shelly's sticky situation," Daniel said. "Shelly was torn between leaving town with Jimmy and staying here with you. She chose you and something inside Jimmy snapped."

"Does Jimmy have a gun?" Olivia asked.

"To be honest, I don't know. When I was running Bo's Place, I always kept a handgun under the counter near the cash register. I took that gun with me when I left town since it was registered to me. I don't know whether Jimmy got one or not," Bo said.

"Wes, get on your laptop and see if you can find out if Jimmy owns a gun," Olivia said.

It didn't matter, Daniel thought. Jimmy could easily kill Rose and Lily without a gun being fired. He suspected Olivia was aware of that, but her command to Wes was an effort to do something, anything.

Lightning once again slashed the sky, closer this time and followed within seconds by a round of rumbling thunder. "What happens now?" Bo asked.

"We wait." Olivia's voice was hollow. "Right now Jimmy holds all the cards. We wait to see what his next move is and then we react."

Daniel knew she was right. There was no way they could act, not with Lily and Rose at risk. At the moment, Jimmy had all the control and until he did something to lose that control, they were in a stalemate.

"No more phone calls," she said as Bo started to use his cell phone again. "We don't contact him. We wait until he contacts one of us."

Daniel gazed at Olivia. Her features were taut, her shoulders back and she appeared in complete command of the situation until he looked into her eyes. There, all of her fear simmered like a bubbling cauldron about to boil over.

Overhead the storm was nearly upon them, the lightning and thunder coming closer and with more frequency. The tempest was reflected in Olivia's eyes, and Daniel feared she'd break before this all came to some kind of an end.

And Daniel couldn't begin to guess how it might end. Jimmy had sounded like a piece of dry tinder about to explode into flames when he'd spoken with Bo.

The minutes ticked by in agonizing increments. Each time Daniel thought of the hostages inside the house, his heart ached with a fear he'd never known before. Although he cared about Rose's well-being, it was the thought of little Lily being terrorized or hurt that made him sick to his stomach.

He couldn't imagine the dark thoughts Olivia must be entertaining as they waited for Jimmy to make some kind of contact.

Although white shades were pulled shut at the front

windows, silhouettes occasionally passed in front of them, letting Daniel know that at least Jimmy hadn't already killed the hostages and then committed suicide as a final end to the standoff.

Wes left his patrol car and returned to where Olivia, Daniel and Bo stood. "Jimmy registered a handgun six months ago, but I called Jimmy's Place and talked to the bartender, who said the gun is under the counter."

"He didn't have time to grab it," Bo said thoughtfully. "Once I confronted him with Shelly's ring, he ran. I chased him down the stairs and he ran right out the back door. It's good that he doesn't have a gun, right?" He looked at Daniel and then Olivia.

"He didn't need a gun to kill Shelly," Olivia replied. Her voice held a tremble that spoke of how close to the edge of a breakdown she was.

Again Daniel wanted to take her into his arms, hold her tight against him and take away her pain. Unfortunately, he knew he wasn't what she needed most at the moment. What she needed was to have her daughter in her arms, safe and sound. What she wanted was her mother out of that house and standing next to her.

He hated that he didn't know what to do, that he didn't know how to resolve this without taking a risk, and he wasn't willing to do anything that might risk Rose and Lily.

The ring of Olivia's phone jarred all of them. She answered and put it on speaker. "Jimmy, you need to tell me how we can solve this so that nobody gets hurt."

"This is what I want." His voice was harsh and it was

difficult to realize this was the same man who greeted them at the bar and grill with a boyish smile and oozing charm.

"I want all of you to pull out, and that includes anyone you have covering the back of the house. I want everyone far enough away that I can get to my car safely," he said.

"We can do that," Olivia agreed. Daniel assumed she was willing to let him drive away from here because she could put out a bulletin to law enforcement outside of Lost Lagoon. He might leave their little town, but he wouldn't get far.

"And for assurance purposes I'm taking Lily with me. When I know I'm safe I'll drop her off somewhere and let you know where she is," Jimmy added.

"No. No way are you leaving that house with my daughter," Olivia replied frantically, and tears began to well up in her eyes.

"That's the only way this will end," Jimmy replied. "I'll give you fifteen minutes to agree to my plan. If you don't, then things are going to go bad in here very quickly." He disconnected and Olivia might have fallen to the ground if Daniel hadn't caught her.

He held her close as she wept—no longer Sheriff Bradford, but simply a terrified mother. Lightning crackled and thunder boomed overhead.

The skies had yet to unleash a torrent of rain, but the rain was on Olivia's face as she wept uncontrollably in his arms. She finally looked up at him. "We have to get them out of there. You have to get Lily out. She's your daughter, Daniel. You have to save her."

He froze and dropped his arms from around her. "What did you say?"

She swiped at her cheeks, and as he stared at her it was as if everything else around them disappeared. "That night in New Orleans…we made Lily. She's your daughter." Olivia choked on another sob. "And now she needs her daddy to save her."

Her daddy. Her age…her bright green eyes so like his own. God, why hadn't he realized it before now? Lily was his child, his own flesh and blood.

He couldn't think about that right now. If he did, he'd fall into a miasma of emotions that would mess with his head. Jimmy had given them fifteen minutes to agree to his demands.

The clock was ticking and somehow, someway he needed to bring this all to an end. Thunder boomed overhead once again, and with it an idea sprang to life in his mind.

"Move all the men back," he said to Olivia. "Call in the men surrounding the house."

"Surely you aren't agreeing to his demands," Olivia asked, her eyes wide with horror.

"No, but I want him to think we're complying with him. Get everyone moved out of the area. Trust me, Olivia. I have a plan but we need to move fast."

It took four minutes to have all of the men leave. They moved to the next street over to wait for further commands. Once they were gone, Daniel looked at Olivia.

"Call Jimmy and tell him you want to see Rose and Lily in the front window, that you won't agree to anything else until you see them with your own eyes."

"And what are you going to do?"

"Hopefully, I'm going to save my daughter," he replied grimly. With these words he raced for the side of the house. With his heart pounding near heart attack speed, he slowly moved around the back of the house and to the other side.

He crouched down beneath the window that he knew was located in Lily's bedroom. He peeked inside to find the room dark. Good. The darkness was his friend.

The unlit bedroom and the storm raging overhead were advantages. But the alarm system was a definite disadvantage. If it had been rearmed after Jimmy had entered the house, then Daniel's plan wouldn't work and the results could be catastrophic.

If he tried to open or break the window and the alarm sounded, then Jimmy would know immediately that somebody was attempting to enter the house.

Jimmy was already agitated and desperate, a dangerous combination. Daniel had no way to guess what his reaction might be. He hoped that Olivia had made the call and if Jimmy complied with her request then all three of them would be in the living room.

With the stealth of a jewel thief, he carefully removed the window screen and placed it against the side of the house next to him.

Lily was his daughter. The words whirled around in his head. Why hadn't Olivia told him when she'd first arrived here? Why had it taken this life-and-death drama for her to spill the secret?

He couldn't think of that right now. He needed to stay focused on the here and now and what he needed to do. With his heart beating a desperate rhythm, he waited for the lightning that would be followed by thunder.

He held his gun in his hand, the butt of it ready to hit the window. As lightning slashed the sky, a crackle of electricity shot through him. The thunder boomed, and at the same time Daniel used the butt of his gun to break the window just above the turn lock.

He held his breath and then shuddered in relief as no alarm sounded. Apparently in the chaos that must have occurred when Jimmy had first entered the house, nobody had thought to reset the alarm.

The clap of thunder had provided the right cover for the sound of the breaking glass. Daniel held his breath and reached in and unlocked the window and then slowly eased it up.

It was only when he'd entered the window and stood in the center of Lily's bedroom that he began to breathe again. He steadied his gun in his hand and moved toward the doorway, which would give him a direct line of vision to the living room.

Once again his breath caught in his chest as he stood just inside the bedroom doorway. If Jimmy caught sight of him, then he knew that all bets were off concerning the safety of the hostages.

He peeked his head around the doorway and saw Rose seated on the sofa, sobbing softly. Jimmy stood at the front window, the shade up, and he held Lily up under her armpits as a shield in front of him.

There was no way Jimmy could have a knife or any other weapon in his hand at that particular moment. It was now or never. Daniel burst out of the bedroom. "Jimmy. It's over."

Jimmy whirled around and Daniel didn't hesitate. He shot the man in his right lower leg. Jimmy screamed in pain and went down and Daniel holstered his gun and rushed to grab a sobbing Lily from the floor.

She hugged him around his neck and wrapped her legs around his waist, clinging to him as she cried. His child. His daughter. His heart clenched tight.

"I knew you'd come to save us, Deputy," she finally said loud enough to be heard above Jimmy's cries for help. Rose jumped off the sofa and embraced both of them.

"Let's get you out of here," Daniel said. He went to the front door, opened it wide enough to slip his hand outside and called, "We're coming out." Taking hold of Rose's hand, he led her and carried Lily to safety.

Olivia stood at the end of the driveway as raindrops were finally beginning to fall. At the sight of Daniel with Lily in his arms, she ran toward them. "Thank God," she sobbed as she took Lily from him. Daniel ushered all of them onto the lawn farther away from the house, away from danger, then used his cell phone to call in the men.

Bo entered the house with several of the other deputies. He looked down at the man who he'd believed had been his friend for so long. "I did everything I could to help you," he said.

"And I resented every handout you ever gave me," Jimmy replied. "I was glad when everyone thought you killed Shelly. I was elated when you decided to leave town. I destroyed you."

Bo smiled grimly and shook his head. "I have a wife who loves me and who I love. I'm taking back the business I built and own. You didn't destroy me, Jimmy. You destroyed yourself."

By that time an ambulance had arrived. Jimmy was whisked away under guard. The doctors would deal with his gunshot wound, and once he was well enough he would stand trial for the murder of Shelly Sinclair.

It was finally over. The crime had been solved. And Daniel had a daughter. Overwhelmed by myriad emotions, he left the scene and got into his car. He sat for a long moment and then started the engine and pulled away.

He needed to think. He needed to process everything. He felt raw and oddly vulnerable. What he needed more than anything was some time alone to figure out what he wanted and what he needed to do as a man with a precious child.

Chapter Thirteen

The cat was out of the bag. That was Olivia's first thought when she awakened on the futon just after dawn. And her timing and delivery couldn't have been worse.

She was self-aware enough to know that part of the reason she'd blurted out the information had been a little bit of manipulation. She needed him to know that Lily wasn't just a child in danger, but rather was *his* child. She'd hoped that would be the incentive for him to go to the ends of the earth to get Lily to safety.

She turned over on her side to face the front window where the sun was just starting to peek over the horizon. The storms from the night before were gone and it looked as if it was going to be a clear, sunny day.

What was Daniel thinking? What was he feeling? Did he hate her for getting pregnant, for telling him about Lily or for not telling him about his daughter the first day she had arrived here?

There was no way of guessing what might be going on in his head, because he had left last night without speaking a single word to her.

There would be no reason for him to follow her into work today. While Jimmy had been loaded into the ambulance, he'd confessed that he had been the person who had attacked her in the parking lot.

He'd believed that if he killed her then, the two-year-old murder investigation would once again become a cold case as everyone scrambled to find out who killed the sheriff. He apparently hadn't been rational enough to know that an investigation into her murder might eventually lead to him.

There was no longer any reason for Daniel to act as her bodyguard. There was no longer any reason for them to spend any time together again. The danger was now gone.

She stumbled up from the futon and over to the counter to put on a pot of coffee. As it brewed she stood at the front window and stared out, her thoughts still on Daniel.

She expected nothing from him. She never had. He could choose to be an active parent in Lily's life and they'd figure things out for custody, or he could walk away and decide to be an absent parent.

At least Lily didn't know. If he did decide not to be a father, then Lily wouldn't live with the sting of that rejection. She had poured herself a cup of coffee and was seated at the table when her mother made her morning appearance.

Clad in a pink flowered duster and with her dark hair neatly brushed, she looked no worse for the wear of the trauma of the night before.

"You're up unusually early," Rose said as she poured herself a cup of coffee and then joined Olivia at the table.

"I just woke up and decided to go ahead and get up." Olivia wrapped her fingers around the warmth of her cup. "I guess I've got a lot on my mind."

Rose looked at her in surprise. "I would think your mind would be wonderfully clear this morning. You've cleared the department from any corruption issues and you solved a crime that has haunted the town for two years."

Olivia smiled at her mother. "We didn't exactly solve the crime. It pretty much solved itself." She took a sip of her coffee and eyed her mother over the rim of her cup. She carefully set the cup back down and leaned back in her chair. "I also told Daniel last night that he was Lily's biological father."

Rose stared at her in surprise. "And is that the truth?"

Olivia nodded. "He was the man at the conference five years ago that I met in the bar and then spent a night with and wound up pregnant."

Rose spooned a bit of sugar into her coffee and stirred, obviously taking the time to gather her thoughts. "Why didn't you tell him when we first arrived here and you recognized him as that man?"

"Because in one of the first conversations we shared he told me he was a confirmed bachelor who didn't want a wife or any children. I knew we were here temporarily, so I figured there was no point in telling him," Olivia explained.

Rose studied Olivia's features for a long moment. "You're in love with him, aren't you?"

Olivia sighed miserably. "I am."

"I've seen it in your eyes when the two of you are together. I know you loved Phil, and he was there for you when you needed somebody, but I also know you didn't feel that breathless kind of passion of true love and that's what I see in you when you talk about Daniel."

"It doesn't matter how I feel about him. He just isn't cut out to be a family man." Olivia sucked in a sigh of misery.

"Pshaw, I've never seen a man more ready for a family than him," Rose replied. "He looks at you the same way you look at him. And a confirmed bachelor wouldn't have taken so many opportunities to eat dinner with an old woman and a little girl. He wouldn't have taken us to that ice cream parlor. He might not know it, but he's definitely a family man."

"None of that matters now," Olivia replied. "I'm sure he hates me now."

Rose frowned. "Why?"

"I don't know, maybe because I was stupid enough to get pregnant."

"There were two of you in the bed that night," Rose reminded her. "If you were careless, then so was he."

"But after I told him and after everything was over last night, he didn't even stick around to talk to me. He just left without saying a word."

"I'm sure everything will be just fine, dear." Rose took a drink of her coffee and then got to her feet. "How about I make French toast for breakfast this morning? I think we all deserve a little treat after the night we had last night."

"Sure, that sounds great," Olivia replied. Leave it to Rose to believe that a favorite breakfast food would magically make everything okay. Lily would be happy to have syrup on the menu for the morning.

Lily. Olivia's heart squeezed tight, making it difficult for her to breathe as she thought of how close she'd come to losing her precious daughter and her mother the night before.

Things could have gone so terribly wrong if Daniel hadn't taken the risk to break into the window and take Jimmy down.

Olivia finished her coffee and then headed for the bathroom to shower and dress for the day. By the time she had finished, Lily was awake and helping Rose with the French toast.

When she saw Olivia, she ran to her arms, and Olivia sat on the sofa for a morning snuggle. "How is my favorite girl this morning?" Olivia asked.

Olivia had spent some time the night before talking to Lily about what had happened. She'd explained that there were some bad people in the world and unfortunately one of them had gotten into the house. Lily had told her mother she'd tried to be brave but she had cried. She'd also told Olivia that she'd known in her heart that Deputy would get inside and take the bad man away.

"I'm good," Lily replied and then smiled impishly.

"I couldn't be bad with French toast and lots of syrup for breakfast."

Like Nanny, like granddaughter, Olivia thought an hour later as she drove toward the station. A little syrup for breakfast made the whole world sweet and wonderful and cast out all the evil in the world.

The closer she got to work, the more her stomach twisted into nervous knots as she tried to anticipate what to expect from Daniel.

Really, all she had to tell him was that nothing had changed. Within a couple of weeks at the most, she and her family would go back to Natchez and he never had to think about them again. Despite knowing the truth about Lily, there was no reason his life had to change at all.

He wasn't at his desk in the squad room when she walked in. She headed for her office amid cheers and congratulations from the men who were present.

Everyone was in high spirits with the closure of Shelly Sinclair's murder case, with the knowledge that the murdered young woman could finally now rest in peace.

She bowed with forced playfulness to the men and then quickly escaped into her office and closed the door. She sank down at her desk and wondered how long it would be before Daniel came in, before there was some sort of a confrontation between them.

It was ten o'clock when she saw, through the blinds, Daniel enter the squad room. He didn't speak to anyone but walked directly to her door and knocked.

He entered the office and immediately closed all the blinds that would allow anyone to see inside the private office. She watched him closely, trying to gauge his mood, but it was impossible.

He finally sat in the chair in front of her desk, his green eyes as mysterious and unfathomable as the depths of the swamps that half surrounded the small town.

"Was there ever really a Phil who was your husband?" he asked.

"There was. He was the kindest man you'd ever want to know. Although I wasn't in love with him, he was crazy about me. I married him when I was five months pregnant with Lily. He promised to love her like his own and he did so until the day he died."

"I understand why you didn't contact me when you first discovered you were pregnant. We didn't exactly take the time to get full names or addresses that night in New Orleans, but why didn't you tell me about Lily when you first arrived here?"

Olivia held his gaze steadily. "Because you wouldn't have wanted to know, because you told me you were a confirmed bachelor and had no desire for marriage or children. I didn't want to burden you with the truth."

He shook his head and raked a hand through his hair, and for the first time she noticed the deepened lines that radiated out from his eyes, indicating a night of little sleep.

"I went home last night and tried to wrap my brain around everything that had happened. I was shocked by Jimmy's actions and the fact that he'd hidden how much he hated Bo and that he'd killed Shelly. But I was completely stunned by you telling me that Lily was my daughter."

"I shouldn't have told you, at least not the way I did. But, Daniel, nothing has to change. I mean, I don't want child support or anything like that. You can just pretend I didn't tell you and go on about your merry way," she said, although each word ached in her heart.

He stared at her as if she'd lost her mind. "Everything has changed. I went home last night and sat in my living room and listened to the silence that lived there. I've always liked the quiet. But, lately, the silence hasn't felt good. In fact, it's been lonely. I've been lonely and questioning the path I'd chosen for myself." He leaned forward in the chair. "I want to be a part of Lily's life."

Olivia's heart swelled. She'd wanted this for her daughter. Daniel was a good man and he would make a wonderful father. "Then I guess what we need to do is talk about custody for when I have to return to Natchez."

"I want full custody," he said and leaned back in his chair. His eyes simmered with a wealth of emotions, but his words caused Olivia's breath to whoosh out of her. The last thing she'd ever expected was a custody battle with him.

"I… You can't…" Hot tears sprang to her eyes.

Daniel leaned forward once again. "Olivia, you didn't let me finish. I want full custody of Lily, but I also want full custody of you and Rose."

"What?" She stared at him, afraid to guess what he meant, afraid to embrace any hope of dreams coming true.

He got up from his chair and walked around her desk. He took one of her hands and pulled her to her feet. "Olivia, I was awake all night long, fighting who I believed I was and what I've become, what you've made me become."

"I don't understand." She gazed up at him, loving him so much it hurt and afraid of misunderstanding exactly what he wanted from her.

"I realized last night that I was a confirmed bachelor because I'd never met a woman who made me want to be anything else. I didn't want children because I didn't care enough about any woman to want to go there with her. What I realized last night was that I wasn't that man anymore, that I had met the woman who made me desire marriage and children and a mother-in-law who is sweet and kind."

She began to shiver as his words sank into her brain and then downward to fill her heart. "I love you, Daniel." The words escaped her.

He cupped her face with his hands. "And I love you. I love you more than I ever dreamed it was possible to love. I want you in my life, Olivia. I want you and our daughter and Rose to build a life together forever."

He stopped talking and instead took her mouth with his, kissing her with a sweet tenderness overlaying a simmer of desire that stirred her in her very soul.

When the kiss finally ended, he kept her in his

arms. "We'll need to figure out how this is all going to work," he said. "I'll quit my job here to move to Natchez. Sooner or later I'll find some kind of work there. I can sell the house and pick up stakes."

She looked up at him. "Or maybe we could just stay here. I could talk to my boss and see about getting transferred here. In fact, I hear through the grapevine that there's going to be a new sheriff elected eventually. What do you think my chances are in getting elected?"

"I think with the right man backing you, your chances are very good," he replied, his eyes shining with the happy confidence of a man who knew what he wanted and where he was going.

"I think if we work together we can accomplish anything, Olivia. But, are you sure this is where you want to be?" A frown appeared across his forehead.

"There's really nothing for me in Natchez, and with the new amusement park going in, things should be jumping here in Lost Lagoon. But, the truth is, I'll be happy anywhere as long as you're by my side."

He kissed her again, and Olivia realized all of her dreams were really coming true. This time when the kiss ended, he grabbed her by the hand and led her toward the office door.

"What are you doing?" she asked.

"We need to hit the road."

"Where are we going?" she asked.

"To your place. We need to tell Lily that she can't call me Deputy anymore. I can't wait to hear her call me Daddy." His eyes glowed with an inner happiness that matched the glow that lit her up inside.

Olivia laughed as they left the office and headed for the back door. As they left the building and stepped outside into the bright sunshine, she knew she was taking the first steps into her future…a future with a man she loved, the father of her child, and it was all going to be magnificent.

Epilogue

Late October was a good time for a barbecue in Lost Lagoon. The intense heat of summer had eased along with some of the heavy humidity. However, the fire of love hadn't stopped burning for Olivia and Daniel.

Olivia now stood at the kitchen window in his house…in their home and watched as Daniel pushed Lily in a swing on a set he'd bought the day Olivia and Lily had moved in with him.

They had tried to get Rose to move in with them, but she'd insisted she wanted to remain in the cheerful little yellow house where she could start a garden in the yard and turn what had been Lily's room into a crafting space.

Over the last month, Rose had made friends with several women, including Mama Baptiste, and the two often met for tea in the evenings and talked about herbs and cooking.

She was still available at all hours of the day and night to babysit Lily, and each Sunday Olivia, Daniel and Lily went back to the little yellow house for dinner.

OLIVIA SMILED AS she heard Lily's laughter. "Higher, Daddy. Push me higher!" Daniel's laughter mingled with Lily's, and Olivia's heart swelled with a love she had never dreamed possible.

A knock on the door pulled Olivia from the window and to the front door. Her mother entered carrying a bowl of potato salad big enough to feed an army.

"Mom, let me help you with that," Olivia exclaimed and grabbed the bowl to carry it to the kitchen, where the table already held burgers and hot dogs ready to be placed on the grill, thick-sliced tomatoes and onions and squeeze bottles of mustard and ketchup.

At that moment, Daniel came in from the backyard, his smile carefree and loving as he looked first at Olivia, then at Rose. "If it isn't my favorite soon-to-be mother-in-law," he said and kissed Rose on her cheek.

"And look, she brought enough potato salad to feed the entire neighborhood even though there are just going to be eight of us," Olivia said.

"But today is a celebration on so many different levels," Rose replied. "And besides, potato salad is always good leftover." She looked toward the window where Lily was still on the swing. "And now I'm going outside to spend some time with my favorite little girl before the others arrive."

The minute she stepped out of the back door, Daniel grabbed Olivia around the waist and pulled her into his arms. "And I'm going to spend a little time with my favorite woman before the others arrive."

As always when he kissed her she tasted his love,

his desire for her and she knew she'd never tire of his kisses. He owned her heart and soul, and each day they spent together only deepened their love for one another.

"Hmm, you taste better than anything that's going to be served today," he said when he ended the kiss.

"That's funny, I was just thinking the same thing about you," she replied.

The doorbell rang, and Daniel sighed as he dropped his arms from around her. "Darn, I was hoping to get another kiss from you, but it appears some of our other guests have arrived."

"You get the door. I still have a few things to finish putting out on the table," Olivia said with a laugh.

Daniel disappeared and returned a moment later followed by Bo and Claire. Bo carried a Crock-Pot of baked beans, and Claire guided him to the table where she plugged it into a nearby wall socket.

"It's a perfect day for a picnic," Bo said.

Olivia smiled. "It's a perfect day to celebrate."

"What can I do to help?" Claire asked as Bo followed Daniel out the back door, where they both hovered over the barbecue pit.

"Absolutely nothing. Just sit and relax. How about a cold beer or something else to drink? I've also got lemonade, sweet tea and soda."

"A glass of sweet tea sounds good," Claire replied. She looked cute as a button with her short curly blond hair framing her face, clad in a pair of denim shorts and a blue sleeveless blouse.

Olivia delivered the tea to Claire just as the doorbell

rang once again. "That will be Josh and Savannah. I'll be right back."

Olivia hurried to the front door to welcome the last of the guests. Savannah carried with her a chocolate cake and as she walked into the kitchen, Josh disappeared out the back door to join the other men at the barbecue.

Olivia looked out the window and then turned to grin at the other two women. "How many men does it take to start a fire?"

"As many as can gather around," Claire replied. "It's a man thing. Wait until they start cooking the meat. It will be utter chaos."

"I don't think Josh will fight anyone over cooking. That man is utterly hopeless when it comes to anything to do in the kitchen," Savannah replied.

Olivia had grown close to the woman who had lost her sister to murder. Since the closure of the crime, Savannah's dark eyes sparkled with happiness and she laughed more often. Olivia was glad that she'd been a part of bringing Savannah the closure she'd needed.

"Before any cooking happens, I want to get everyone together for a round of toasts," Olivia said. She moved to the back door and called for everyone to gather in the kitchen.

It took several minutes for all of them to gather and have drinks in hand. The men all had beer and the women had sweet tea. Even Lily had a glass of grape juice to raise for the toasts Olivia wanted to make.

For a moment as Olivia looked around at the people, her heart swelled with peace and contentment that had ruled her life since Daniel had proclaimed his love for her.

Since Jimmy's arrest, she had formed friendships with Claire and Savannah and had developed admiration and affection for both Bo and Josh.

"Daddy, can we drink now?" Lily asked Daniel.

"Not yet, your mother is apparently gathering her thoughts," Daniel replied.

"I hope she hurries 'cause I'm hungry," Lily replied.

"Okay," Olivia said with a smile. "I just wanted to take a moment and celebrate the fact that Bo no longer lives beneath a shadow of guilt and has reopened Bo's Place."

"Do we drink now?" Lily asked.

Daniel shook his head and Olivia continued. "And I want to celebrate Josh and Savannah's recent marriage and that she's rented space on Main Street to finally open her restaurant."

"Now?" Lily asked with a hint of impatience.

Olivia shook her head. "I'd also like to mention how happy I am to have been elected sheriff of Lost Lagoon last week." Olivia paused a moment, remembering how honored she'd been that the town wanted her to stay, that they trusted her to be the head of their law enforcement and that the powers that be had allowed her to transfer to Lost Lagoon.

"And I took the job at the amusement park and handed in my resignation at the sheriff's department," Daniel added in an obvious attempt to hurry things along. "And Olivia and I have set a wedding date for

December twelfth and I think that's everything. And yes, Lily, now you can drink."

Everyone laughed and raised their glasses and bottles to each other. Love and laughter continued throughout the barbecue. It was nearly bedtime when everyone finally left, Lily had gone to spend the night with Nanny and Olivia and Daniel were alone.

Olivia was at the sink washing up the last of the dishes that wouldn't go into the dishwasher when Daniel came up behind her and wrapped his arms around her as he nuzzled the back of her neck.

"It was a great day," he said.

"It was a wonderful day," she replied and pulled her hands out of the soapy water and reached for a towel.

"It's going to be a wonderful night, too," he whispered.

She turned in his arms and smiled up at him. "I was hoping for a nightcap of some kind."

He kissed the tip of her nose. "When you were making all your toasts you didn't mention the other thing we have to celebrate."

One of her hands fell onto her stomach. "It's early and I still want to savor this particular secret just between us for a little while longer."

She rubbed her hand over her tummy. She was a month pregnant. This time it was planned and wanted and Daniel was by her side.

"Lily will be over the moon when we tell her she's going to get a little brother or sister."

"Just imagine a trip to the ice cream parlor times one million on a chart of excitement," Olivia replied.

"Like father, like daughter," he replied. "This time I won't miss a minute of being a father."

"I love you, Daniel." Her heart was filled with her love for him. He was a kind, patient and loving father to Lily. He'd taken to fatherhood naturally.

"And I love you. I love our life together and the fact that you made me realize the man I was meant to be," he replied.

"Now…about that nightcap?"

His eyes fired with hot desire and he grinned at her. "Far be it for me to keep the new sheriff in town waiting." He took her by the hand and led her out of the kitchen and down the hallway.

The hot, sexy uncommitted man she'd met in a bar five years ago was gone, transformed into a man who embraced love of his daughter, his soon-to-be mother-in-law and her. It was no longer a fantasy she entertained, it was a reality she lived…and loved.

* * * * *

INTRIGUE

Available February 16, 2016

#1623 NAVY SEAL SURVIVAL
SEAL of My Own • by Elle James
Navy SEAL Duff Calloway's vacation turns into a dangerous mission when he meets Natalie Layne. She is in Honduras to rescue her sister from human traffickers—not to fall in love with a sexy SEAL.

#1624 STRANGER IN COLD CREEK
The Gates: Most Wanted • by Paula Graves
Agent John Blake is hiding in Cold Creek to recuperate from gunshot wounds. He never expected to thwart an attempt on Miranda Duncan's life—or to find himself falling hard for the no-nonsense deputy.

#1625 GUNNING FOR THE GROOM
Colby Agency: Family Secrets • by Debra Webb & Regan Black
PI Aidan Abbot is undercover as Frankie Leone's fiancé to clear her father's name. But the closer he gets to the truth, the more Aidan wants to protect the woman he was never supposed to fall for.

#1626 SHOTGUN JUSTICE
Texas Rangers: Elite Troop • by Angi Morgan
When a serial killer targets Deputy Avery Travis, it is up to Texas Ranger Jesse Ryder to protect her. But he'll discover that falling for his best friend's little sister is almost as dangerous as the killer stalking them.

#1627 TEXAS HUNT
Mason Ridge • by Barb Han
The man who once traumatized Lisa Moore is back—and he's deadly. Lisa turns to her childhood friend, Ryan Hunt, who risks his life and heart to help. But can Lisa ever truly escape her past?

#1628 PRIVATE BODYGUARD
Orion Security • by Tyler Anne Snell
Bodyguard Oliver Quinn can't deny his history with his new client, PI Darling Smith. But keeping her safe from a killer comes before exploring their lingering feelings.

REQUEST YOUR FREE BOOKS!
2 FREE NOVELS PLUS 2 FREE GIFTS!

H HARLEQUIN®

INTRIGUE

BREATHTAKING ROMANTIC SUSPENSE

YES! Please send me 2 FREE Harlequin® Intrigue novels and my 2 FREE gifts (gifts are worth about $10). After receiving them, if I don't wish to receive any more books, I can return the shipping statement marked "cancel." If I don't cancel, I will receive 6 brand-new novels every month and be billed just $4.74 per book in the U.S. or $5.49 per book in Canada. That's a savings of at least 12% off the cover price! It's quite a bargain! Shipping and handling is just 50¢ per book in the U.S. and 75¢ per book in Canada.* I understand that accepting the 2 free books and gifts places me under no obligation to buy anything. I can always return a shipment and cancel at any time. Even if I never buy another book, the two free books and gifts are mine to keep forever.

182/382 HDN GH3D

Name	(PLEASE PRINT)	
Address		Apt. #
City	State/Prov.	Zip/Postal Code

Signature (if under 18, a parent or guardian must sign)

Mail to the **Reader Service:**
IN U.S.A.: P.O. Box 1867, Buffalo, NY 14240-1867
IN CANADA: P.O. Box 609, Fort Erie, Ontario L2A 5X3
**Are you a subscriber to Harlequin® Intrigue books
and want to receive the larger-print edition?
Call 1-800-873-8635 or visit www.ReaderService.com.**

* Terms and prices subject to change without notice. Prices do not include applicable taxes. Sales tax applicable in N.Y. Canadian residents will be charged applicable taxes. Offer not valid in Quebec. This offer is limited to one order per household. Not valid for current subscribers to Harlequin Intrigue books. All orders subject to credit approval. Credit or debit balances in a customer's account(s) may be offset by any other outstanding balance owed by or to the customer. Please allow 4 to 6 weeks for delivery. Offer available while quantities last.

Your Privacy—The Reader Service is committed to protecting your privacy. Our Privacy Policy is available online at www.ReaderService.com or upon request from the Reader Service.

We make a portion of our mailing list available to reputable third parties that offer products we believe may interest you. If you prefer that we not exchange your name with third parties, or if you wish to clarify or modify your communication preferences, please visit us at www.ReaderService.com/consumerchoice or write to us at Reader Service Preference Service, P.O. Box 9062, Buffalo, NY 14240-9062. Include your complete name and address.

HI15

SPECIAL EXCERPT FROM

♦HARLEQUIN®

INTRIGUE

Read on for a sneak peek of
NAVY SEAL SURVIVAL,
the first book in
New York Times *bestselling author* **Elle James**'s
SEAL OF MY OWN *series*

Setting herself up as bait is the only way for
Natalie to find her abducted sister. But all her
training can't prepare her for the irresistible stranger
she must trust with her life.

He looked up, hoping to see Natalie at the surface, thirty feet above. She wasn't there. His heart racing, Duff hurried through the rocks. Where the hell was she?

Movement ahead made him kick harder. As he neared a large boulder, he saw fins kicking and flailing. The smooth, pale legs attached could be none other than Natalie's.

When he was close enough he could see that a man had hold of her around the neck and was feeding her a regulator. He had her arms wrapped in what appeared to be weight belts, her wrists secured behind her.

Anger spiked, sending a surge of adrenaline through Duff. He raced for the attacker, holding his knife in front of him. He'd kill the bastard if he hurt one hair on Natalie's head.

Natalie's attacker must have seen Duff. He shoved Natalie toward him and kicked away from them.

Duff grabbed her from behind and held her against him. She fought, twisting her body in a frantic attempt to get free.

Finally, Duff spun her to face him, pulled the regulator from his mouth and shoved it toward hers.

She stopped struggling and opened her mouth, accepted the regulator, blew out the water and sucked in a deep breath.

Duff turned her, slipped his knife between her wrists and sliced through the heavy weaving of the weight belt material, taking several passes before he freed her hands.

When she was free, she grabbed hold of his BCD and anchored herself with him. Natalie took another deep breath and handed the regulator to him.

They buddy-breathed for a couple more minutes until she was once again calm.

A shadow floated over them, indicating the location of the boat. One by one, they surfaced and waited their turn to climb aboard the boat.

Duff surfaced a second before Natalie.

When she came up, she spit her regulator out of her mouth and gulped in fresh air. She glared across at him. "Why the hell did you do that?"

He frowned. "What do you mean? I saved your life."

"I wasn't dying."

Find out what happens next in
NAVY SEAL SURVIVAL
by New York Times *bestselling author Elle James*

Available March 2016 wherever
Harlequin books and ebooks are sold.

www.Harlequin.com